MAN TRACKERS

The gunman had done his best to stick to rocky ground and spots where there was little snow left. However, it hadn't been entirely possible. Perhaps recognizing that, he had finally taken to a small glacial stream that had already thawed. There the trail ended. Dolf looked up the hill, then down. "I'm bettin' he ain't up there. Let's try the other way."

No tracks emerged from the stream at any point all the way down to the lake. The rivulet flooded out onto the lake ice, covering it for several hundred yards with a few inches of water.

"Just on a hunch, let's head toward that other camp and see if our friend's tracks show up somewhere," Dolf said.

They were rewarded at last with a set of tracks along the shore. In the slush, they couldn't be sure they were the same tracks, however. Even Thunder wasn't certain. "I tink mebbe so," he said. "Mebbe no. No good."

"What do you think, Doc?"

"Can't say. Let's circle around and pay those guys a visit anyhow. They'll be watchin' for us to come this way if they're watchin'."

MORGETTE IN THE YUKON

G. G. BOYER

LEISURE BOOKS   NEW YORK CITY

A LEISURE BOOK®

June 2001

Published by

Dorchester Publishing Co., Inc.
276 Fifth Avenue
New York, NY 10001

ISBN 0-8439-4886-8

Visit us on the web at www.dorchesterpub.com.

CHAPTER 1

THE justifiable suspicion around Ft. Belton, Montana, Territory was that someone was going to die pretty soon. Anyone who knew Dolf Morgette knew that. And the whole community knew Morgette. Not that he was a cold-blooded killer, though his enemies were apt to say that. But he had killed—as a lawman—and he'd killed outside the law when he'd been driven to it in a range war over in Idaho. As marshal of Ft. Belton, he'd had to kill "Shootin' Shep" Thompson just that past summer. Shep had had a reputation something like Wild Bill Hickok's. As chief of the town's underworld, Shootin' Shep had felt compelled to brace the new marshal. In the wry concensus of the community, he had died "of a plain overdose of bad judgment."

Killings in the West had a way of leading to more killings. Shootin' Shep's taking off had undoubtedly led to the later back-shooting of Dolf's friend Harvey Parrent. Harvey hadn't been what the West called a "fighting man," but he had been a scrapper. That had led to the fracas in which Thompson was killed. The circumstances had had all the earmarks of a setup to get Dolf whipsawed and kill him. Thompson's partner, Rudy Dwan, had picked a fight with Harvey's younger brother when he and Harvey had unsuspectingly stopped in Dwan and Thompson's saloon for a beer. The knowledgeable all read that as a situation cut out to bring the marshal to the rescue on the run, since the Parrents were greenhorn "hoemen" from Minnesota whom Dolf had taken under his wing. That strategy had backfired on its perpetrators because Harvey had quickly taken over the scrap for his younger brother and proceeded to knock hell out of the much bigger Dwan, to the amazement of everyone there, especially Rudy himself and his partner. As a result, rather than being ready for a sneak shot at Dolf when he came through the bat-wings as expected,

5

Shootin' Shep was busy covering Harvey Parrent with a six-shooter to keep him from wading back in and really cleaning up his half-whipped partner, Dwan.

Dolf, suspecting what might be afoot, had slipped in quickly, pistol ready, sized up the situation in a flash, and snapped, "Freeze, Thompson!"

Shootin' Shep was an old hand at that sort of affair. He knew when the break was going against him and had folded his hand. Dolf had gently suggested, "Just ease that six-shooter down, Shep, and set it on the bar nice and slow and easy."

"Okay, Dolf. I was just tryin' to break up a little trouble."

Dwan had struggled to his feet groggily and wobbled over to the bar. Dolf's sense of danger had warned him the trouble wasn't over yet. He darted his eyes around for someone possibly ready to sneak a shot at him. This had given Shootin' Shep the cue he'd needed to make the move that had always worked for him before, snaking a derringer from his vest pocket. He learned that he'd picked the wrong man just before Dolf's .45 slug tore into his heart, spinning him around and slamming him to the floor, dying.

"Too fast!" had been his last panicky thought.

Dwan had then foolishly tried to take up the play, going after Shootin' Shep's still-cocked six-shooter on the bar. Dolf, still covering Thompson in case he might be alive yet, hadn't seen this move. But Gabriel Dufan, who had been having a beer down the bar, had. He had hurled his beer mug with all his might at Dwan, scoring a perfect hit that had knocked him out cold. It had been a move that was to make for Gabriel a lifelong friend.

Dufan hadn't stepped into the affair as a total stranger. He had already helped Dolf and the Parrents locate homesteads. He was agent for Mayor Ira Baker, who had hired Dolf as marshal. Baker was also the town's leading merchant and real estate developer. He'd hired the two Parrent brothers as teamsters till spring, when they could put in their first crop.

As soon as Baker heard of the shooting, he'd warned the Parrents, "You boys had better steer clear of Dwan from now on. He'll be lookin' for his first chance to get even—not so much over his partner gittin' killed as over losin' face." He'd chuckled at a sudden afterthought. "Losin' face in more ways than one, I guess." Then he'd got serious again. "You watch out too, Dolf. The rough crowd'll be meek as lambs to your face from now on, seein' what you did to their big cheese, but watch your back. They tried Old John Hedley that way a couple of times when he had your job—ended up pushin' up daisies for their trouble, but their kind never learn. Besides, you can never tell when they'll get lucky. It only takes once."

Ira had proven a prophet in more ways than one. The town had got so quiet by fall that Dolf had felt no qualms about joining Gabriel Dufan on a brief foray to Canada to help a friend in dire need. He'd have gone in any event, being a Morgette—Dufan had saved his life. He'd have resigned and let the town go hang if need be.

Harvey Parrent had been drygulched just before Dolf and Gabriel returned. Harvey had been out working alone at the time, trying to get Dolf's cabin up before winter. No one would have criticized him for putting up his own cabin first. He'd left behind a wife and five kids with a new one on the way. Nonetheless, it hadn't been his style to think of himself first. And his wife, Julia, had come off the same bolt of cloth. Julia had practically adopted Dolf's young wife, Margaret, and hadn't raised an eyebrow over the fact that she was an Indian—true, an educated Indian who spoke better English than any of them, but nonetheless an Indian among whites in a country that generally held them in contempt.

Harvey'd felt compelled to explain why he'd ignored the Morgettes' natural protests. "It's Margaret's first kid. That's special for a woman. Oughta be born under your own snug roof." He wouldn't hear of anything else either.

So the community rightly expected a killing, and under the

circumstances could hardly wait for it to come off. There'd been small doubt in anyone's mind who the prime candidate was: Rudy Dwan.

Obviously Dwan, whether guilty or not, would draw the same conclusion. Not surprisingly, he'd disappeared by the time Dolf had got back.

A cold, choking anger had filled Dolf, actually causing a constricted hurt in his chest as he'd stood helplessly at the graveside, grimly watching the pregnant and weeping Julia Parrent with her five doleful, red-eyed orphans. He'd awkwardly tried his best to console the sobbing widow after the short ceremony was over, while the mournful sound of the first shovelfuls of dirt had commenced.

"I'll get the skunk that did this, Julie," he'd promised, "You can bet I'll get him if it's the last thing I do."

"Rudy Dwan did it!" she'd exploded raggedly between sobs. "I know he did; everyone knows it. Harvey beat the puddin' outa him and he just had to get even."

Dolf had already got an idea where he'd find Dwan. Ira Baker was a man with many secret sources of information. He'd told Dolf, "A little bird done told me your man may be on the way to Alaska."

"Alaska?" Dolf had repeated, puzzled.

"Yup. Good place for a feller tryin' to make himself scarce."

That sure had made sense. Dolf himself had more than once considered heading for Alaska in times past. It was a place where men usually went for only two reasons: because they were chasing something—usually the rainbow—or being chased.

"What makes you think Dwan is on his way there?" he'd asked.

"Well, I got ways of knowin' a lot of things," Ira had said evasively. "In this case, I think he's been hired by my biggest competitors, those two slippery skunks Brown and Shadley. I think they want him to look after a new little game they're startin' up that way. You know Old John Hedley went up there when he left here. He's runnin' a tradin' post at some damn place called Dyea. What you don't know is that I bankrolled that deal. The fur trade is dead here. He's makin' a mint at it for us up there."

He paused to let that soak in, carefully clipping and lighting a cigar. "Anyhow, that country's opening up. Me and John was figuring to put a steamboat on the Yukon and give the Alaska Commercial Company some competition in the interior. As I get it, Brown and Shadley have the same idea. The competition could get pretty rough. I think they got Dwan to go up there to take care of the shootin' if there is any—and there will be. How'd you like to hire on to handle the same kind of job for Baker and Hedley?"

"I'm your man if you're reasonably sure Dwan will be up there."

"I'm sure," Baker told him, meeting his eyes squarely, "damn sure! Sure of something else, too. The Mounties have a good notion who was with Dufan when he went up to bust Henri Lemoine outa jail in Saskatchewan. I'd guess in a few weeks—long enough to get the papers through Washington —the U.S. marshal here in Montana is gonna want a little talk with you about an extradition hearing. You got more to worry about than Gabe, since President Cleveland gave him political asylum. That don't mean the Mounties won't try to have someone deliver you *both* the other side of the line. They've pulled abductions off before through friends here that make a lot off their business. Both of you'd better cut out for a while. If you was in Alaska, they'd have a hard time talkin' to you, much less takin' you in. There ain't no marshal up there yet, or much of anything else either according to Hedley."

For those reasons, Dolf, Gabriel, and the pregnant Margaret ended up headed for Portland, Oregon, on the NPRR. The Morgettes were about to join some of the few Americans who had gone to Alaska before the goldrush.

Dolf grinned affectionately at the sight of his big friend, Gabriel Dufan, peacefully sleeping across the aisle, slumped down in a seat. He had learned to love the big sentimental Métis half-breed during their short, abortive Canadian rescue caper. They'd tried to save Gabriel's friend, Lemoine, from an unmerited trip to the gallows for causing a pint-sized rebellion in an attempt to solve the Métis land problems with Canada.

Unfortunately, someone had tipped off the Mounties about a possible rescue attempt, and the guards had been heavily reinforced at the last minute. Gabriel and Dolf had ridden for it, pursued by numerous redcoat patrols. One had jumped the two fugitives just at first light one morning, well inside U.S. territory, near the Bearpaw Mountains. They had been forced to flee bareback, abandoning all their equipment. Dolf grinned again, recalling the immediate aftermath.

"Dem Cochan sumbitch!" Dufan had sworn. "You bet me I get my tam saddle back."

He'd been as good as his word. The Mounties apparently hadn't expected the two to circle back and follow them, assuming they'd be relieved simply to have outrun the pursuit. Two of the patrol had been left to slowly follow the rest, bringing Dolf's and Gabriel's equipment with them. The first warning these two had got was Dolf's command, "Hands up!"

This had been where Dolf discovered an unexpected sense of humor in his big half-breed companion, who'd insisted on taking the Mounties' trousers as well as their own saddles and equipment back.

Dolf could still hear the futile protest of one saying, "Oh, I say, this is deucedly uncricket."

He suspected that the redcoats' interest in interviewing him and Dufan might be tinged as a result with an ambition to recoup their "sacred honor," or something equally British.

So now Dolf was, in a sense, a fugitive. He also knew he had to go after Dwan, whether Dwan might be the lucky one that would finally get him or not. But neither of these considerations bothered him. There was another matter troubling him deeply. It touched his heart sorely and recurred to his mind again as he tenderly watched his little Margaret. She was at that moment curled up on the opposite seat with her head pillowed on his rolled-up coat, sleeping peacefully as a kitten.

Only the spring before, she'd nursed him back to life when he'd been wounded and near death, hidden in the camp of Chief Henry, her father. He'd got well and gone to settle his score with those who had tried to kill him, and he'd won. He'd won everything, that is, but what he'd wanted most: lovely Victoria Wheat. Bitterly disappointed—over a total misunderstanding, as he now knew—he'd left Idaho alone at night, intending never to return. Through all this, Margaret had shadowed him, never in sight, but always watching. And that bitter night she'd made her presence known. Grateful, vulnerable, and no longer lonely, he had accepted what she offered, and being an honorable man, when they had encountered the Indian missionary, Father DuFresne, Dolf had got him to marry them.

He almost laughed out loud now, remembering the first night of their honeymoon. Lying in their robes looking up at the stars with her head nestled on his arm, he'd suddenly said, "Now, Margaret. I've got you. You've got to love, honor, and obey me." A long silence had followed. Then she'd blurted out, "Phooey!" and, laughing like a little demon, had rolled over and attacked him. The tussle had ended in a passionate embrace. Their idyll had ended because of his need to seek a living for them, with her child on the way. They'd gone to Ft. Belton, where he'd gotten the marshal's job.

He recognized now that his loneliness, rather than love, may have impelled him to want to marry her. This had come to him with great poignance when he'd received a letter before they'd left Ft. Belton. It read, in part:

My Darling Dolf,
We all wondered where you had gone till we read in the papers that you were marshal there.
I have waited long to get up my nerve to write to you. I must be a woman first and speak my heart. You must feel

*about me as I do about you if what your grandmother
surmised of your departure is true. You were so wrong in
what you must have thought when you came to see me
that last night and must have seen me impulsively kiss
Alby Gould for all he had done for us. . . .*

*Dolf, I love you deeply and hope you feel the same way
about me. I will be here waiting for you, and waiting for
a letter even before you come home.*

*Ever yours with love,
Victoria*

He had never sent the expected letter. And he knew he
wouldn't come home for a long time, if ever. Yet he kept her
letter. This had been as bad as Harvey's death. He didn't love
Margaret as he had Victoria, yet he knew he would always stay
with her.

Someday, I might go home, he thought. He had always
wanted to start his own ranch. It had been his intention to
ranch from his homestead at Ft. Belton, rather than farm as
the Parrents had aimed to do. Maybe after Alaska, he
thought. Maybe then we can go home to Idaho. Victoria will
probably be married by then and have forgot all about me.

Reflection on Alaska turned his mind back to Rudy Dwan.
"I'll catch up to him," he thought grimly, "and when I
do. . . ."

CHAPTER 2

WHEN Dolf, Margaret, and Gabriel reached Portland on the NP, it was early December, the weather lowering and misty. Dufan left for San Francisco by coastal steamer the next day, planning to lay low there, since he had a sister living in the Bay City.

There were tears in the big Métis's eyes as he bid Dolf and Margaret good-bye at the gangplank. He kissed Margaret impulsively on the cheek, then in typical Gallic fashion held Dolf by his shoulders, looking him straight in the eyes. He smiled broadly, his black eyes still teary. "We meet again someday, my fran," he said. "Py gar, you one damn fine big sumbitch, Dolf."

Dolf grinned, shook hands warmly, clapped Gabriel on his rocklike shoulder, and said, "You too, Gabriel. We'll miss you. I hope our paths do cross again. And—I'm sorry we couldn't save Henri."

Lemoine had been hanged just after they'd returned from Canada. Gabriel shook his head once, impatiently, tears welling again in his eyes, then spun and rapidly stumped up the gangplank. At the top he turned, waved, then disappeared on board.

"Do you think we will ever see him again?" Margaret wondered.

"I hope so. He's been a good friend."

Dolf spent the next couple of days outfitting for the arctic, not being certain how much of their necessities he could obtain at Juneau or Dyea. Having punched cattle in country that sometimes dropped to forty below, he had a fair idea of what was needed. He was particularly concerned to be sure Margaret would be warm and comfortable. Their child was due in March. He'd considered holing up somewhere until nearer spring since he couldn't start on Ira Baker's Alaskan

13

project until then anyhow. He decided against it for what he deemed good reasons: his own need to lay low and the fact that Margaret would have to make the trip either far along in her pregnancy or with a small child. Perhaps the most compelling argument for a quick departure had been that there was no better place for a fugitive than Alaska, which he'd been told had no civil law as yet.

In any event, Ira had instructed him to report to John Hedley at Dyea, saying he'd arrange a place for the Morgettes to live.

He hadn't forgotten Rudy Dwan either. Getting him in a set of gunsights was something Dolf itched to do. He wasn't vengeful, but he recalled all too clearly the picture of five tearful orphans and a widow standing dolefully in a row beside Harvey's grave. Even in the unlikely event Dwan hadn't killed Harvey Parrent—one of the finest men who ever drew breath —Dolf wasn't forgetting Dwan had tried to kill *him* in that sneaky manner after he'd killed Shootin' Shep.

I'll give him a chance to come clean if I run him down, Dolf thought. Provided he sings quick, and doesn't try any of his underhanded tricks while I'm doin' it. And I *will* run him down sooner or later.

Before he'd left Ft. Belton, Dolf had managed to get a good picture of Dwan from the portrait studio there since they'd kept plates on file of everyone they'd photographed. In Portland he'd hit paydirt in practically the first place he'd shown the photo—the outfitter's where he was getting his Alaskan supplies.

"My cousin," Dolf had explained in order not to arouse suspicions that might impel someone to mention an over-curious stranger to the police. "If I missed him here, he's supposed to meet me up north." He'd been deliberately vague about *where* up north.

"Sure," the clerk told him after looking at the photo. "Big fellow. Was in a week or so back. Bought about the same kind of stuff you're gettin'. Didn't say where he was headed, but we can pretty much figure that out in here from what they buy. By the way, there's a fellow in the back right now it wouldn't hurt ya to talk to—Jack Quillen. We see him almost every winter or two. C'mon back and meet him."

Quillen was a rangy, bearded redhead with a stubby pipe clenched firmly in one corner of his mouth. He proffered Dolf a big horny callused hand that had recently done a lot of pick-and-shovel work, Dolf guessed.

The clerk introduced Dolf as Adolf Morgan (the cover name he was using for obvious reasons, with a well-advertised reputation such as his). Dolf was happy that other customers drew the clerk away from them since he wanted to ask Quillen if he knew Hedley.

"Old John and me are sorta partners," Quillen stated. "He grub-staked me to go look over some prospects fer 'im last year. Good man. Straight as a string an' ain't skeered o' the devil himself. He's got the Injuns up there skeered plumb peaceful practically single-handed. Hung a couple of 'em personal fer killin' his clerk over not lettin' 'em have some likker. Funniest damn thing ever happened. A boat full of greenhorns stopped just as Old John strung up the first one. Yuh kin bet their mouths was wide open when they pulled in an' that was the first thing they saw, since Old John used the hoist on the dock to do the job. Took John a couple o' hours to run down the second Injun in the brush. Jist as that same boat was pullin' out, Old John swung off the second Injun. Yuh could 'o knocked the eyes off that crowd on the boat with a stick. Some damnfool newsman came back down here an' wrote we wuz hangin' them pore Injuns jist fer fun."

Dolf took a quick liking to the bluff Quillen, who was a mine of information about Alaska.

"Cold. Keerist, it gets cold, 'specially when the wind's cuttin' at a feller. But a man can dress for it an' if it's too cold dig in and siwash it out." Dolf discovered from Quillen that "siwashing" meant camping out like the Indians, digging into a snowbank if necessary to get out o' the wind. "Just like the grouse," Quillen explained. "They fly up a ways, fold their wings, and dive straight into the snow where it's loose enough."

Quillen had looked over Dolf's list. "Yuh got almost everything you'll need. Could git it up north, but it'd cost a lot more. Git a short-handled shovel an' a saw, though. That's how we do like them grouse. Dig in. If the snow's packed, yuh kin cut it in blocks with a saw an' build a house to git outa the wind. Git a whisk broom, too. To brush snow outa yer 'parky' when yuh git where it's warm. Otherwise it'll melt an' freeze when yuh go back outside. If it does, 'twon't keep yuh warm worth a hoot anymore. Jist the opposite."

Dolf learned that a 'parky,' as Quillen called it, was a parka, the fur overgarment with a hood that was the principal north-country outer garment in winter.

"Keep yuh warm at sixty below," Quillen said. "But don't git 'em down here. Git an' Injun-made one up at Hedley's. Got wolfskin hoods that won't frost up when yuh breath on 'em.

"By the way, if yuh ain't got one, git a .45-90 Winchester. Them big brown bears is plumb hostile. They ain't the least bit skeered o' humans. We git somebody killed 'r mauled every season, 'specially in spring when they're jist outa hibernation an' real hungry. I see yuh got snow glasses. Cain't do without 'em or you'll go snowblind sure as hell. If you do an' you're out alone, you'll be a goner."

Dolf was pleased when he discovered Quillen was booked north on the same boat as he and Margaret, the small steamer *Idaho*. He wanted to learn more from this seasoned north-country veteran, especially why someone might want to start a second, much less a third, steamboating operation in such a sparsely settled locale.

The *Idaho* was remarkably well appointed, having twenty compact staterooms as well as many bunks in open bays. Captain Magruder was an old friend of Quillen's, which fore-stalled any problem over shipping Dolf's horse Wowakan at that season. He was put in a stall specially knocked together for the trip and swung into the hold with a cargo boom, followed by several bales of hay. Jim Too, the hound, was stowed down there with him, looking aggrieved over the proceeding.

"Yuh can get plenty more hay for 'im in Juneau," Quillen allowed. "Lots o' hosses an' mules in the mines and the logging business around there. Hedley keeps a team up at Dyea, too."

While Wowakan was being loaded, they were joined by Cap Magruder, as everyone in the North called him.

"Just about to pull out, Cap?" Quillen greeted him.

"Just about. Waitin' for a package. Got some medicine comin' for a special passenger. Russian nobleman born up at Wrangell, sick an' goin' home to die. Came on board last night on a stretcher with his own private doctor. Up in Cabin A, the big one."

"Carryin' a full load of passengers?" Dolf asked out of idle curiosity. It seemed he'd seen a lot of them come aboard just since he and Quillen had been out on deck.

"Pert near. Got ninety-seven. We can carry a hundred without crowdin'. More if we want 'em packed like sardines. Surprised to see this many goin' back north this time o' year."

"Gold," Quillen opined. "Some o' us got a nose fer it. The next big diggin's'll be up north, mark my word. Besides lots of 'em come outside fer a spree, went busted except fer their boat ticket. Goin' home to live on tick off the likes of Old John Hedley, or their sidekicks, or try to get put on in the woods."

"How we goin' this trip?" Quillen asked.

"Inside. It's runnin' forty foot high outside," Cap said. "Two or three overdue a week, maybe lost."

Noting Dolf's puzzled look, Cap explained, " 'Inside' is inside the islands. Called the inland passage. Lots calmer seas this time o' year. Sometimes make better time outside, but not in winter. Runnin' out there the propeller's out o' the water an the bow's in on every wave. Inside you'll get to see some real scenery. We'll be in sight o' land the whole way. Besides, we won't have everybody seasick—includin' yore hoss," he added as an afterthought.

"You ever seen a glacier, Dolf?" Quillen asked.

"Nope. Not except in a picture book."

"You'll see plenty of 'em. An' most likely seals and sea lions and whales. Whales seem to like to run alongside and look over boats."

"Margaret'll get a kick out o' that."

Just then she was down in their cabin napping. She got tired easily these days but had an enormous, healthy appetite.

"Here comes our package," Cap interrupted. "We'll be underway pretty soon." He left them, headed for the bridge.

Dolf was glad to be alone with Jack Quillen. He'd looked for a chance to pump him for anything he might know about Baker and Hedley's plans for steamboating on the Yukon and the rationale behind it. He'd already told Quillen why Baker was sending him to Alaska and had debated telling him who he really was.

Better wait on that, he cautioned himself. First appearances are sometimes wrong. He liked Quillen a great deal and in just a couple of days had come to trust his judgment. But you could never tell on short acquaintance just which side a man's bread was really buttered on.

Dolf opened the subject obliquely. "What do you suppose a smart fellow like Baker is doing sending the likes of me north to get him in the steamboat business when I hardly know one end of one from the other?"

Quillen eyed Dolf speculatively. "Maybe he figgered you got special talents he thinks they'll need. Besides, Old John Hedley was steamboatin' on the Missouri fer ten years before he went ta tradin', then lawin'. What he can't tell you about the business won't be worth knowin'. They'll need extra hands they kin trust."

Dolf grinned. "It sounds like you might know more about this business than I thought."

Quillen winked. "You kin bet on it, Dolf."

"You wouldn't by any chance know who I am, would you?" Dolf tried him on a hunch.

"Yup. An' I wasn't standin' over in the outfitters by accident the other day either. My orders was to see if you were really goin' through with the deal before I spoke up. The gangplank is comin' up, so it looks to me like you're our man. Wait'll we get out a ways where there ain't so many people millin' around an' we'll have a confab somewhere. Not in any o' these cabins, though. You kin hear through the walls. We're onto somethin' big up north and the competition knows it—I wouldn't put anythin' past 'em, even on board the *Idaho* here. So keep yer eyes open. I'll be around later."

Quillen moseyed off up the rail, relighting his pipe. Dolf decided to go down to their cabin to see if Margaret wanted to watch them get underway. The *Idaho*'s whistle emitted two sharp blasts just as he turned and headed below, the steam drifting downwind and quickly evaporating. Low ragged clouds had started to spit a cold mist.

He found Margaret peacefully asleep in the lower bunk under a quilt, looking untroubled as a small child. The cabin was far from commodious. In addition to the two bunks, it had a clothes rack with space for a trunk under it and a washstand. There was a single porthole. A bracket lamp beside the mirror over the washstand provided the only light. Heat was rumored to circulate through a radiator; Dolf wondered if it would. It was chilly in the cabin now. He worried that Margaret might not be able to stay warm as they moved farther north.

Two more blasts on the whistle didn't even cause Margaret to stir. She was sleeping so soundly and peacefully he decided not to rouse her. Instead he climbed into the top bunk, arranged a blanket over him and was soon dozing. He was awakened a couple hours later by someone knocking at their door. Before he was fully awake, Margaret got up and opened it. Quillen stood in the passageway.

"You two'll miss grub if you don't get a hustle on," he said.

"I don't want to do that," Margaret laughed. "If I get seasick, I don't want to be hungry, too."

"You won't," Quillen assured her.

Dolf could feel their motion, a gentle swell as yet, although they'd cleared the mouth of the Columbia and were actually at sea. He experienced a faint queasiness as they moved down the companionway, and his eyes told him the ship was rolling one way while his balance told him it was just the opposite. The feeling departed as soon as they hit the cold air on deck and he regained reference to a reliable though faint horizon in the rapidly fading light. The dining room and galley were amidships right on deck.

Dolf was happy to see that Margaret's wolflike appetite was still with her. He'd been worried she might get terribly seasick and lose the child. However, his earlier attempt to persuade her to follow him only after the baby came had netted him an emphatic "No," followed by a stony silence. Now he was glad she'd come. He thought, She's going to be the sailor of the two of us. The thought was reinforced by the fact that what little he could get down didn't sit too well. He was happy to get back on deck.

He asked Margaret, "Would you mind if I join you later? Jack and I want to talk over some things out here where we can't be overheard."

"I'll turn off my ears. Did you know us squaws can do that? I'll bet you didn't." Then, sensing his disapproval, she said, "It's nice out here. You two stand down the rail far enough away so I can't hear. I'll be inhaling this fresh air," she added, taking in a huge breath of it.

She saw their faces in the matchlight as Quillen lit his pipe and Dolf got a cigar going. She was relieved to see that; she'd thought perhaps he might be getting seasick and knew he would be embarrassed, and also knew she'd have wanted to suffer his embarrassment for him.

"Ever hear of Sky Pilot Fork?" Quillen asked Dolf.

"Can't say I have."

"I'm not surprised. Few outside of the Yukon country have, most likely."

"What is it?"

"Well, there's a story behind it. A missionary went through the country about five year back a-tryin' ta save the heathens 'n when he came out with his hair still on—which suprised everybody—he had a sack full of big gold nuggets. Only he wasn't interested in gold, he said, just souls. He'd picked 'em outa a creek someplace, just because he thought they was pretty, but he couldn't remember where. Didn't even have ta pan 'em, he said. They was so big and shiny he just plucked up a bunch with his fingers in a couple o' hours one afternoon. Well, the boys just about hung him when he couldn't come up with the foggiest idea where he'd been. They named the place the Lost Sky Pilot Fork, and we all went lookin' for it." Quillen paused like a good storyteller ought to, puffing to get his pipe going good again.

"Anybody find it?" Dolf asked, as he realized he was expected to.

"Nope—that is, not till last summer."

"Who?"

"Me."

One thing became immediately clear to Dolf. If a big new gold discovery came in, there'd be room for a lot of steamers on the Yukon. He could foresee cutthroat competition while the moneyed interests jockeyed to seize economic control. The need for a man of his particular background in the "steamboating" business became crystal clear.

To confirm his suspicions, Dolf asked, "Where do I fit into this deal?"

"You're gonna go in with me and stake these claims. You're gonna keep me alive after we do it. It's big. There'll be a new town crop up overnight. And you're gonna be the law along the Yukon till the army gets around to movin' in or they send us some marshals. That'll take a couple of years, at least. The boys'll back you to the hilt with miner's meetings, if I know 'em, in case we need to hang somebody or somethin'."

Dolf grinned, although Jack Quillen couldn't see that. "What about my steamboats?"

"Leave that to Baker and Hedley. The boats'll be upriver to meet us. They already got the stuff layin' up at St. Michael to build 'em before spring. You'n me'll go over Chilkoot Pass before spring breakup and build us some boats to go down the Yukon the other way and stake them claims."

"How about my hoss?"

"We'll build a barge for 'im. We'll have lots of time to talk before this tub gits to Dyea. Let's join the little lady before she gits a bun on at yuh—I know gals. Used ta have one of my own."

After learning what he had from Jack Quillen, Dolf looked over all the male passengers closely the next day, alert for any familiar hardcases. Quillen's news made it probable Dwan's backers would be bringing in more just like him. Although there were a few frosty-eyed articles that looked like a hard winter, Dolf couldn't place any of them.

The *Idaho* glided up the coast through six ideal sailing days, the weather having broken clear their second day out. Margaret was a joy to watch, exclaiming over the whales Jack had said they'd see, and marveling over the glaciers and towering white mantled mountains that dropped almost straight into the sea.

Jack spent several hours every day slyly educating Dolf on the things he'd need to know to survive in the arctic.

"It's plumb beautiful up there," he said, "and damned unforgiving. Make one mistake and you're a goner, maybe froze to death, maybe drowned, might get 'et by a big brownie. I've even knowed of one case where a feller was killed by mosquitoes. I noticed you had about a quart of Citronella. You'll need it. Head nets an' gloves, too. O' course, after you're up there awhile you'll jist go without baths as long as the Injuns do an' mosquitoes'll let yuh alone. Even bears don't git downwind o' Injuns if they can help it. Cain't say as I blame 'em. Wait'll yuh smell one o' them villages fer the first time. Keerist!"

That's the way the education went. Mostly Quillen put everything in a whimsical frame, but there was always a solid nub of essential information at the heart of what he had to say.

"You'll have to learn to mush a dog team too. We'll start hardenin' yuh up fer that this winter. Gotta be able ta break trail all day on snowshoes. Gotta learn what ice is safe an' what ice ain't. Same with snow over crevices.

"Might have ta have Margaret knit that big dog o' yours a sweater this winter. But he looks ta me like he's got some wolf cross in 'im. Maw nature'll knit him a sweater next winter. He's big enough to make a sled dog if he's tough enough to stand off the other dogs. Most of 'em are part wolf. Yuh gotta show 'em who's boss 'r your own team might jump yuh."

Their last night at sea, after Margaret had turned in early, the two had a final chat.

"I'm gonna turn in," Jack said.

"Me too, as soon as I finish my cigar."

Dolf strolled to the fantail, enjoying the starry night. It had been remarkably mild the whole trip. The turbulent water from their propeller appeared faintly luminous. Dolf took a final puff on his cigar and watched its fiery arc snuffed out as it hit the water. He was startled to be struck alongside the head by something at just that moment. Stunned, he slumped to the deck, dazedly wondering if something had fallen on him from the pile of excess cargo lashed behind him on deck. His head was just beginning to clear as he sensed that someone seemed to be trying to help him up. It was a big man, hustling him up along the railing by his armpits. Then he realized what had happened. Vaguely he recalled that the sound of a shot had been audible above the thum thum of the propeller and the rush of water under the stern.

Shot me, the thought flashed through his mind. Now he's tryin' to toss me overboard.

Realization of mortal danger cleared his mind instantly. He spun and struck the other in the midsection as hard as he could, driving him away. Unfortunately, Dolf's violent exertion caused him to slip and fall on a faint scum of frost that coated the deck. As he fell, he jerked his pistol from a shoulder holster. His attacker may have seen or anticipated this move. He had spun away and was running, scurrying out of sight behind the bulky deck cargo. Rapidly as Dolf regained his feet and pursued, no one was in sight when he cautiously looked around the nearby canvas-draped pile of stuff. Dolf thought of rousing Cap Magruder and conducting a search. Then he thought, What the hell for? It could've been almost anyone —except our Russian nobleman.

He very cautiously made his way back to the cabin, holding his handkerchief to his wound. He held the door open wide to let the companionway light in to be sure no one was laying for him there.

He had to light the lamp to patch up the gash on his head. This woke Margaret. Seeing the blood, she was out of the bunk in a flash.

"What happened?" she asked, her eyes mirroring her deep concern.

"I slipped on the ice."

To keep from getting any more blood on his Mackinaw and shirt, he had peeled down above the waist to his underwear. Margaret held a balled handkerchief to his wound and got her first good look at the gash. She knew from the experience of one whose people had fought the Army what a scalp wound made by a bullet looked like.

"Someone shot you," she said.

"Not only that," he said. "Tried to throw me overboard."

"Does your head ache like you might have a concussion?" Margaret asked.

"It doesn't feel good. But just bandage me up and let me get some sleep. I don't think it busted my thick skull."

She insisted on putting him in the bottom berth. He was too weak to argue. When he woke up, they were already docked at Juneau. Jack Quillen finally came around when they didn't show up on deck. Margaret hadn't slept much herself, but she didn't want to rouse Dolf before she had to. Jack's arrival took care of that. Dolf told him what had happened.

"No sense in squawkin' to Cap. We couldn't pick that guy out. I didn't get much of a look at him. No idea who it was."

"Want me to go borrow that Russian's stretcher?" Quillen asked, half-jokingly. "He was the first man off. I watched 'em takin' him down the gangplank, bundled up to his eyeballs."

Dolf got up and tested his legs.

"I'm fine," he said. "There is one thing I'd like you to do, though. I thought of it just before that geezer shot me."

"You name it."

Dolf produced his picture of Dwan. "How about showin' that to Cap. Shoulda done it myself before now. We don't know that Dwan's actually here yet. He may pick the *Idaho* to come on if he ain't. Cap can let us know if he does."

Quillen departed on that errand while Dolf and Margaret got their cabin things ready to depart. They had a two-day layover in Juneau before them since the *Idaho* didn't go to Dyea. Jack was back in remarkably short order looking like a man bursting to tell a secret. He handed Dolf his picture of Dwan.

"You ain't gonna believe this, Dolf. That damn Russian nobleman was Dwan. Cap got a good look at him the night they brought him on board."

"I'll be damned! At least we don't have to guess who took that shot at me. What's the chance of finding him in Juneau?"

"None. If he's got friends—and he sure as hell has—he'll be out in the woods by now holed up in somebody's cabin."

CHAPTER 3

"HOW beautiful," was Margaret's response to Juneau's setting. The hills rose abruptly from the water's edge, densely forested, towering above the raw, growing village. The weather had been comparatively mild and rainy, but snow nonetheless capped the surrounding mountains. Scattered stumps could be seen here and there around the muddy townsite, revealing the newness of the five-year-old settlement.

Jack Quillen seemed to know everyone in town. He'd gone ahead uptown to get rooms for their two-day wait for another steamer that would be going to Haines and Dyea, then returned for them. Meanwhile Dolf had got Jim Too from the hold and had been assured by Cap that he would get Wowakan safely ashore later.

Strolling uptown, the three passed a large log structure which a sign proclaimed as the Skookum Saloon. A large malamute jumped up from where it had been laying on the porch, bristling and growling at Jim Too. Dolf's attention was attracted by a man in gambler's garb standing just inside the front door; the man uttered a low-voiced "Sic 'em," probably thinking he wouldn't be heard.

The malamute shot off the porch and made a wild leap at Jim Too, looking utterly baffled as Dolf's big dog deftly sidestepped him. The malamute, obviously an experienced scrapper, spun around to close again. Jim Too dodged behind him with lightning swiftness, guided by the instincts and courage of a good hunting dog. His huge jaws clamped on a rear ham of the other dog and set like a vice. The malamute was heavier and spun Jim Too with him every time he lunged, but this caused the hound to be just out of his reach each time. At first the malamute snapped angrily, snarled, and growled, then dawning fright caused him to yip like a frightened pup.

The sound of the fight attracted several spectators from

nearby businesses as well as the Skookum Saloon itself, including the sneak who'd sicced the dog on Jim Too in the first place. He rushed out with a stick of stove wood, aiming to club Dolf's dog. Quillen deftly tripped him, and he sprawled in the mud cursing. He jumped up and grabbed at his shoulder holster, but stopped at the sight of Dolf's six-shooter, which had almost magically appeared under his nose—he couldn't even tell for sure where Dolf had drawn it from.

"That'll do," Dolf told him calmly. "We heard you sic your dog on him. Now get a hold of his collar and I'll get mine off of him."

The gambler meekly followed orders.

Quillen addressed him, "Still up to your old snide tricks, Goldie—I'd think you'd learn."

Goldie gave Jack a dirty look as he led his thoroughly cowed malamute away, limping badly and bleeding. They disappeared together into the Skookum.

Dolf reholstered his pistol, and the three continued up the street a ways when something impelled Dolf to glance back. Goldie was just coming back out on the porch with a shotgun.

"Get behind me," he ordered Margaret. Dolf couldn't be sure whether the gambler was after him or Jim Too. He didn't redraw his pistol, however, since Goldie was holding the shotgun pointed down, perhaps simply planning to get off some mouth to save face. He'd learned Goldie's type sometimes were best handled by letting them bluster. Slowly the gambler started to raise the muzzle, obviously intending to shoot either him or Jim Too.

"Hold it right there," Dolf ordered in a cold voice. Something in the tone suggested to Goldie that he'd better do as he'd been told.

"You can't hit me at that range with your peashooter," Goldie blustered.

Dolf grinned coldly. "You look like a gamblin' man, podner. I'll go you a double eagle I can put one in that wood ball on top of the post next to yuh."

Goldie's eyes wavered, glancing out of their corners at the fancily turned ball Dolf mentioned.

"You're on," Goldie finally agreed.

The pistol again snaked out as it had before, rose just as swiftly, flashed, roared, and the ball splintered into a hundred pieces, all in a split second, some of the slivers showering Goldie. Before the gambler recovered his wits, Dolf was walking rapidly toward him, the smoking pistol dangling down at his side.

"Put the shotgun up," he suggested mildly. "I'll take my twenty."

Flabbergasted, Goldie leaned the shotgun on the porch railing and sheepishly fished out the gold piece, handing it to Dolf.

"The show was worth the price, stranger. Mind if I ask who you are?"

"Name's Morgan," Dolf told him, sticking to his cover. "Thanks for the twenty."

He turned to rejoin Margaret and Quillen. Like Jim Too, he knew when he had his dog whipped; there was no need to look back this time. Goldie was still rooted where he'd left him, mouth open, staring after Dolf's retreating figure.

"Hey, Quillen, wait up," someone yelled from behind them.

The three stopped and turned.

"Oh oh," muttered Quillen. "The sheriff. Probably heard the shootin'. Let me handle him."

The lawman arrived, puffing a little but trying to look dignified.

"Meet our sheriff, folks. Paul Brown. Paul, this is Mr. and Mrs. Morgan, friends of mine. He's goin' to work for John Hedley."

The sheriff shook hands with Dolf.

"I saw that shootin'," he said. "Normally I'd give a man hell—pardon me ma'am—give a man heck, for shootin' in town, but I'd say it was sure justified in this case. That was some shot. I was gonna ask you how you'd like a job as my deputy, but I probably can't match Hedley's wages. Anyhow, the offer stands." Turning to Quillen, he explained, "I'm expectin' a peck o' trouble. Caldwell hired a bunch of China-men, an' the boys over at his mine are goin' out on strike. They say they're gonna run all the chinks outa town. If that's all they do, I don't aim to take a hand, but I'm bound to have to step in if they go to lynchin' anyone, even a chink."

"Caldwell's a dern fool if he asked fer that kinda trouble," Quillen stated.

"Anyhow," Brown said, "your stay shouldn't be dull. I suppose you're waitin' for the steamer up to Dyea. By the way, John Hedley's in town somewhere himself."

He raised his hat to Margaret, looked at Dolf again, and said, "Offer's good anytime for a man can shoot like you, Morgan."

"Thanks," Dolf said. "I won't forget."

"Oh—and watch out for Goldie Smith. He don't forgive or forget easy."

"I'll second that," Quillen said as they resumed their course. "He owns the Skookum. His games are all crooked. They used to call him the king of the conmen back in the Rockies some-place, can't remember where. He must be onto something about our game, too. Told a friend o' mine, John King, he expects there'll be a big strike someday up in the interior, and when the boom camp grows up there he aims to be boss. Offered King the job as chief of police when the time comes; he used to be a cop. Can you imagine? King told him he must be on the pipe."

From a second-floor window of the Skookum, behind slightly opened shutter slats, Rudy Dwan had watched the dog fight and its aftermath. He hadn't met Goldie himself yet. Some of Goldie's men had smuggled him off the boat and into the Skookum that morning. He recognized the man outside from descriptions he'd got.

Observing Goldie's having to eat crow at Dolf's hands, Dwan muttered under his breath, "Damn fool."

He'd figured that Brown and Shadley's kingpin up here

would be a real smooth operator. Goldie didn't impress him as that. But then, Rudy thought, nobody told me he was the real big cheese, just told me to check in with him for instructions. Another thought entered his mind: Morgette is greased lightnin'; not only that, but the best shot I ever saw. We'll never get him from the front . . . but we'll have to get him sooner or later, nonetheless.

His line of thought was interrupted by the arrival of Goldie. Dwan didn't intend to be the first to mention what had just happened outside.

"You know anything about a gunslinger named Morgan?" Goldie asked.

"Why?" Dwan asked.

"I just had some trouble with him outside."

Dwan grinned unpleasantly. "You mean the guy out front just now with the big hound?"

"That's him."

"His name ain't Morgan."

"What the hell is it?"

"Morgette. Dolf Morgette."

"Jeezuz! So that's Dolf Morgette. I shoulda known. I'm lucky to be alive. Did you see that shootin'?"

"I saw it. Seen it before. I was there when he killed Shootin' Shep Thompson. There ain't a man in the West could take Morgette in a fair fight. I saw Thompson kill two or three men, an' I thought he was good. Morgette killed him before he got half-started. He's plain poison."

"I been told he's lookin' for you."

"That goes two ways."

"You'd better hope to hell you don't find him where it's light."

"I damn near got him last night on the boat."

Dwan related what had happened. He neglected to mention the very bad night he'd spent afterward in his cabin praying that Dolf didn't have the boat searched and somehow divine that the Russian nobleman was a clever blind. He hadn't drawn an easy breath till the man posing as his doctor and the pair Goldie had sent to meet him had spirited him safely away to the Skookum. This was his first chance to talk with Goldie since Goldie, like most gamblers, was a late riser. Here at the Skookum, Dwan himself had got his first sleep since taking that shot at Dolf. The recent racket out front had interrupted his nap.

"At least you tackled Morgette the savvy way, from the back at night, but you knew who he was," Goldie defended his recent fiasco. "It wouldn't be easy any other way. I doubt if we could get anybody even willing to gang him if they know who he is. He'd take too many with him, even if they got him. But sooner or later he has to be put out of the way."

"I know," Dwan said. "The main reason he took a job up here was probably because he knew I'd be here." After he revealed that, he quickly wished he hadn't. He saw the calculating look cross Goldie's face.

"What'd you do to him?"

Dwan hesitated, then hedged. "He thinks I killed a friend o' his."

"Did you?" Seeing the nasty look come over Dwan's face, Goldie quickly added, "Never mind. It's none of my business. But I'm glad to hear gettin' him out of the way is a groundhog case with you. Quillen is a different proposition. We've got to keep him alive."

"What the hell for?" Dwan asked.

It suddenly dawned on Goldie that Dwan hadn't been let in on the Lost Sky Pilot story; certainly not all of it. He wondered why, while hastily covering up.

"Maybe I hadn't better tell you just yet," he evaded the question. "But whatever the hell you and the boys do from here on out, don't beef Quillen till I give the word."

Goldie shuddered to think what would happen to him if he somehow allowed Quillen to be disposed of before they learned his secret. If they couldn't get the truth out of him by some means, the plan was to follow him when he went over in the

Yukon country to stake the district, which he surely would do as soon as the spring ice breakup permitted. Putting two and two together, it was obvious to Goldie that Baker and Hedley had employed Dolf to keep Quillen alive after he'd located and staked the Lost Sky Pilot.

To Dwan he said, "You hadn't better show yourself outside this room except after dark, at least till Morgette goes on up to Hedley's, which I expect he plans to do."

Dwan nodded his agreement.

"But I got a job for you and a couple of the boys after dark. If you get a chance, I want you to sap Quillen and kidnap him. I want him sweated for some information."

"What information?" Dwan asked suspiciously.

"Didn't they tell you?"

"Twead was the only one I talked to in Ft. Belton before I left. He said you'd fill me in on everything I needed to know. I wasn't lettin' any grass grow under my feet when I pulled out of there, you can bet."

Goldie thought about the proposition for a moment. Maybe it *had* been left solely up to him. In any event he didn't see how Dwan would be much use to them if he didn't know what they were after from Quillen. After all, he'd been told Dwan was to be the kingpin of his muscle squad just as Morgette apparently was for Baker and Hedley. Accordingly, he decided to fill the big thug in on the Lost Sky Pilot story.

He concluded by saying, "Twead was intercepting Baker's mail from Hedley through a connection at Ft. Belton. Otherwise we'd never have learned that Quillen finally found the right creek last summer. When the news breaks, there'll be a thousand men stampede in there from all over. Our outfit aims to get the lion's share of that plum—furnish the transportation, supplies, and the works. I aim to control the gambling and likker trade. And maybe we can work out something even better'n that between us." He waited for Dwan to rise to the bait.

Rudy's avaricious nature prompted an immediate curious response. "What might that be?"

"Depends on how much you love your bosses back in St. Louis."

Recognizing what he was expected to say, although Goldie could be testing him, Dwan risked the truth—but evasively, just in case.

"About as much as they love me, I reckon."

"In that case, maybe we can work out a little sweetheart deal. Those business dudes are interested in makin' money only off business. They ain't in our class when it comes to brass. My idea is that some of that gold might occasionally get lost, strayed, or stolen on the way outside. There could be half a million or a million in a big spring cleanup if the diggins turn out as rich as I think they might. It's got to go out on the river steamers."

This proposition set Dwan's mind to work in earnest. Is this guy on the level? he wondered. He'd seen personalities like Goldie's before. Half real stupid, half very smart, but entirely dangerous in either case.

"I may be your man," Dwan said. "I just could be the man you're lookin' for. Now how about this deal with Quillen? If he's moseying around loose, I'll get him for you. Easiest thing in the world if the fellow isn't expecting it."

CHAPTER 4

QUILLEN had got their lodgings at a square two-story hotel that looked just like the standard design Dolf had seen in every little western town he'd been in. In fact, Juneau reminded him of Pinebluff except for its setting by the ocean. He'd been surprised to find the weather at this time of the year milder than back home in Idaho. He'd never heard of the moderating effect of the Japanese current along the southern coast of Alaska and the West Coast in general.

Right then, he was concerned to get Margaret something to eat and a warm place to rest.

"How yuh feelin', honey?" he asked her, offering her his arm up the porch steps.

She smiled gratefully up at him, then turned and surveyed the town they'd just traversed.

"I'm just fine. The excitement didn't bother me at all, if that's what you mean. I ought to know by now you can take care of yourself—and me. Us, I should say," she added, smiling again and patting her by now fairly large belly. "I just love the smell of the ocean air mixed with balsam. And the country is breathtaking; it looks like someone stood it on end." She swept her arm around in an arc to emphasize that she meant the whole bowl of mountains surrounding the town and the Lynn Canal.

Dolf was smiling indulgently as he turned to the door and held it open for Margaret. The lobby's warmth, radiating from a large German heater in its center, was welcome even though it wasn't freezing outside.

"Here's Hedley," Quillen announced as a man came purposefully down the stairway.

Hedley was a tall, heavy-set, broad-shouldered man with iron gray hair and beard, and deepest steely blue eyes that regarded everyone directly, appraisingly, from a florid face.

"You'd be Morgette," Hedley said without introduction, holding out his hand. Looking at Margaret, he didn't have to say what he was thinking. "Hello," he acknowledged her presence; then to Dolf he said, "Married to a Sioux myself." Hedley was no diplomat. He meant: "So we're both squaw-men, how about that?"

Margaret smiled inwardly, unoffended. She took an instant liking to Old John, as everyone called him. She could see Dolf becoming Hedley in another twenty years, only she'd bet Dolf would be less brusque. She hoped the years never changed Dolf, remembering the arm he'd given her up the steps the moment before.

"Let's talk," Hedley said as soon as they'd registered.

"We ain't et yet, John," Quillen told him. "The little lady's probably starved, not ta mention yore old pard here. Somethin' that cain't wait?"

Impatience crossed Hedley's face briefly. Then he erased it. He usually didn't stand for objections to his own desires, or even whims, but he was as fond of Quillen as he'd ever been of any man.

"Suit yourselves. I got a couple of little errands to do. Why don't I see you afterwhile. It ain't anything that won't keep an hour or two." He left abruptly, striding rapidly as he always did, bent slightly forward and looking like someone about to butt his head through a wall.

The clerk looked slightly surprised when Dolf took Jim Too down the hall with him to their first-floor room, but he made no comment. Margaret noticed the look and whispered to Dolf, "He probably saw you educating Goldie down the street and decided to treat you with kid gloves. Almost everybody came out for the dog fight and the shooting."

Dolf only grinned.

Quillen went on down to his own room. "See you in the dining room after I wash up," he called back. "Incidentally, I told the clerk to have our stuff put in the rooms when Cap sends it up from the ship."

Margaret sank down on the bed with a sigh. Then she laid back on the pillow and stretched.

"Mmm," she uttered a little luxuriating sound. "This bed is comfortable. I was tireder than I thought. I get poohed out so easy carrying your son."

Dolf turned from the washstand and eyed her amiably. "You keep saying that. Maybe it'll be a girl—suppose I want a cute little daughter that'll grow up to be like her pretty maw?"

Margaret looked him over severely; then, imitating her father's best ceremonial manner, she gravely intoned: "Uhn! All great warrior want boy child!"

Dolf crossed the room, carefully sitting down on the edge of the bed beside her and enfolding her in a careful embrace, then gently kissed her. She kissed him back fiercely, then thrust him away suddenly.

"You can squeeze me harder than that. Your son won't mind. He knows somebody loves us."

Dolf drew back and looked her in the eyes with such great serious intensity, even sadness, that she became alarmed.

"You're thinking something sad," she accused. "I won't have it, not when I'm so happy. What is it, Dolf?"

He was silent, regarding her with sober tenderness for a long while. Finally he said, "I hope we always love each other is all. Life sometimes does things to people they can't help."

She knew about his first marriage and its tragic consequences. She sensed that this was what he was thinking about. Dolf had lost his father and older brothers, murdered in a range war. Later, after a revenge clean up of the Pinebluff District in Idaho he'd been framed and sent to prison. His wife Theodora's testimony would have cleared him but may have sent her lover, Sheriff Ed Pardeau, to jail instead. That had been Dolf's first inkling of his wife's unfaithfulness. He'd had five bitter years in prison to reflect that Theodora, whom he'd deeply loved and unquestioningly trusted had put him there. Finally pardoned he'd been almost killed going after his family's murderers. Ultimately he'd had to kill Ed Pardeau and drive political czar Mark Wheat out of the country.

His life had been one tragic or bloody mishap after another for almost a decade, leaving him deeply scarred and even more deeply mistrustful of women in general. Margaret knew she had partially overcome the latter bitterness; she'd nursed him back from the brink of death and gladly followed him into his self-imposed banishment. She'd seen him gradually emerge from his protective shell, at least where she was concerned.

"Life won't manhandle us," she said, heedlessly trying to throw off the mood induced by reflecting on his sad past. "I'll always love you, Dolf."

He took her in his arms again, this time more roughly. But he was thinking, It's not you I'm worried about, honey. He was glad she didn't know about the letter from Victoria Wheat buried in the bundle of papers in his trunk, a letter he found too dear to throw out.

His unhappy mood had passed by the time they joined Quillen in the dining room.

"Ever have moose stew?" Quillen greeted them.

"Yup," Dolf said.

"Me too," Margaret chimed in.

Quillen looked disappointed. "I forgot you two came from moose country. Better try the caribou then."

They all laughed over Quillen's finding something Alaskan to top them with after all.

After the meal, Dolf escorted Margaret back to their room, then rejoined Quillen for more coffee and a cigar.

"Lord, that little lady can pack away the chuck," Jack observed. "Does a man's heart good to see it."

"Eatin' for two," Dolf said. "She says she's feeding our son who will grow up to be a mighty warrior—like his daddy," he added slyly.

"Don't joke," Quillen replied, suddenly serious. "You are a great warrior, whether the likes of Dwan and Goldie would like to admit it or not. Wait'll old Goldie finds out someday who he tried to brace this mornin', an' he'll likely get a case of the vapors and keel over. We're countin' on you to keep this deal together, Dolf, so we don't all lose out. Brown and Shadley are a couple of St. Louis dudes from what we get from Ira Baker's letters, but the kind they'll hire and look the other way will be no joke. This operation really needs you, so you can count on 'em tryin' to git you again, sure as death and taxes."

"I'll be on the lookout," Dolf assured him. "I've gotta keep you in one piece, too, or nobody'll be able to find the Sky Pilot's diggins."

"They know that, too," Quillen pointed out, just as Goldie had to Dwan. "Nobody's gonna touch a hair of my handsome head till I lead the way to the big bonanza. Then it'll be too late. The big fight after that'll be over who's gonna be head hog at the trough."

Just then Hedley burst in the same way he'd left—rapidly, purposefully, looking as though his head couldn't wait for his feet to get him where he was going. He swung a chair around and nervously straddled it backwards, his arms folded on its back, fingers drumming.

Without preliminaries, he burst out, "I had my safe blown open just before I left. After your map, I suppose, the damn fools, as if I'd keep one there if I had one. I was up on the pass helpin' rescue some idjit comin' out this time of year."

Was it possible, Dolf wondered, that neither of them had a map and that the whole deal depended on Jack Quillen staying alive? If so, he had a hell of a big responsibility, especially to Ira Baker, to keep Jack alive.

"I'm glad you're here, Morgette," Hedley was saying. "By the way, I want to convey the world's thanks for making it a better place to live in."

Dolf looked at him, puzzled.

"You beefed one of the rottenest sons-of-bitches that ever

lived—Shootin' Shep. I'd bet he hired every one of the low-lifes that tried to back-shoot me when I was marshal up at Ft. Belton. Him or Rudy Dwan."

"Dwan tried to get Dolf on the *Idaho* last night before we docked," Jack told him. He related the whole story and why they surmised it was Dwan.

"Well, I'll be go to hell. So he's actually up here. I've had folks on the lookout. Mighta knowed he'd sneak in. No tellin' where he's holed up. I wouldn't put it past Goldie Smith to be hidin' him over at the Skookum. Been an unusual number of hardcases hangin' around there lately. Somethin's in the wind over there. Most likely though, Caldwell's got himself some strike breakers. Hired some chinks, too, but the boys are fixin' to put 'em on the *Idaho* tonight an' send 'em back outside. Oughta drown the bastards. With Dwan around, we oughta go over to the Skookum jist on the off-chance he's holed up with Goldie, kick in all the doors on them upstairs rooms, and shoot the bastard if we find him. Goldie, too." He grinned over another thought. " 'Course if we got the wrong room, some o' them gals'd squawk, but my notion is we'd save ourselves a lot of trouble. On second thought, though, those lacy-pants bastards in St. Louis would jist send up another bunch of hardcases we didn't know. Dwan's a sonofabitch, but at least we know what his pasty phiz looks like. He'll turn up soon enough, probably when we least expect him." He changed the subject abruptly. "By the way, Morgette, I got you and the wife a snug cabin all ready. You can stable yore hoss with my team. I got plenty o' feed, too."

Then he pointed to Jim Too, who was lying asleep on the floor at Dolf's feet. "Your dog?"

Dolf nodded.

"I heared he crippled Goldie's big malamute. Haw! Good thing he can handle himself. He'll have to whip his way through my twelve or starve to death. I got two dog teams. This country's jist catchin' onto dogsledding. I picked it up from the Cannucks up in the Whoop Up country in Canada. Best way ta travel in winter. We'll make a dog man outa ya before we're through."

"Amen," Quillen agreed. "Your life can depend on your dogs. By next winter you'll be an old hand at it. Better be."

Hedley spent considerable time describing his plans for the coming season. Much of it Dolf already knew or had surmised.

"You and Jack will move over to Lake Bennett before spring breakup. I'll get some boys to help you whipsaw out some boats. I don't reckon anyone'll bother you before Jack actually starts locatin' claims. That is they won't bother Jack, at least. Dwan and Co. know why you're up here, Dolf. You'll have to watch your back every second."

"While you fellers are going in that way, I'll have another crew slappin' together our first steamboat at St. Michael. Already got the material up there. I'll be comin' up on it with a load of trade goods to meet you and pick out a townsite on the river handy to the diggins."

That, in a nutshell, was the Baker-and-Hedley partnership game plan for the next year.

"It looks to me like the key to your operation is keeping Jack here alive," Dolf said. "Which means I gotta keep me alive, which I'm sure always interested in doin'. And especially now that I'm about to be a papa again."

As he said it, a fleeting thought passed through his mind of his other two children back in Idaho—Dolf Jr. and his younger sister, Amy. He missed them and wondered if he'd live to see either of them again.

He heard Hedley telling Jack, "I don't figure you're in any danger for now. Dwan'll know you're the key to his bread and butter, too, regardless of what he may try later. But keep your eyes open anyhow. Stick close to me or Dolf, I'd say. Now, I've got a hundred things to iron out around town. I'll see you two for supper and maybe a leetle touch of the creetur afterwards. We oughta go over to the Skookum and give old Goldie the fantods wondering if we came to shoot up the place. He knows

I don't have any use fer him. After the showin' up Dolf gave him, it'll be more o' the same. Of course," he added to Jack, revealing an unexpectedly dry sense of humor, "I realize you and him are pretty thick."

Jack guffawed. "Ya, in a pig's ear we are."

Hedley rose, formally shook hands, and swept out at his usual gallop.

"Now that," Jack said, "is a four-dollah pistol if I ever saw one." Then, switching the subject, "What're your plans for now?"

"I'm gonna go change the patch on my skull, then catch forty winks with Margaret if she's still snoozin'. If she's awake, we may take a stroll an' see Juneau."

"Watch your back," Jack cautioned. "I may catch some shuteye myself. Also got some chores to do before we head up north. Might's well get at some o' them if I wake up in time."

"Want me to go along?"

"The lady might object."

Dolf laughed. "Like that, eh?"

CHAPTER 5

"DO you drink, Dolf?" Hedley had asked when Dolf rejoined him and Quillen.

"Not much," Dolf had said around the cigar he was firing up. "One whiskey's a good limit in my trade. I have a beer or two occasionally."

"Good. Good. I never drank much when I was in the law business. Still don't, as a matter of fact. But I was serious about the three of us dropping in at the Skookum. I wanna look over the crowd. Something fishy has been shaping up there lately. Besides, it'll make that little bastard Goldie nervous. He'll wonder what we're up to. Especially if he's got Rudy Dwan stashed upstairs."

The Skookum had a long bar in the front room flanked along the opposite wall by gambling layouts. The large back room was occupied by tables and a stage for variety acts. It also had private boxes overhead except above the stage.

Old John, Dolf, and Jack found a spot in the very front of the building where the bar abutted one wall. It was a strategic location with a wall behind all of them and a clear view of the entire front room and part of the theater. The games weren't operating full blast. In the back a few girls were working some miners for drinks. It was a familiar frontier scene. Everyone knew the girls were probably drinking tea or, at best, heavily watered whiskey. Everyone also knew that for a price the girls would go up to a private box when a show was playing, or to a room anytime. It was the most honest part of the operation unless some enterprising girl took it upon herself to roll a customer too drunk to protect himself. The sucker seldom called the law when he sobered up. Most didn't want to show themselves up as fools, and the girls knew it. If some poor sport lost a big poke and squawked, the sheriff usually put the

42

culprit on the next boat, provided a miners' meeting decided she deserved it.

The miners' meeting was the most common form of frontier law where regular civil government machinery hadn't been set up yet. Sometimes the army stepped in to establish order in the Alaskan coastal communities, although forbidden by law to act as a *posse commitatus*. For a miners' meeting, the sheriff would call a jury, and the group would appoint prosecutor and defense counsel (not necessarily trained lawyers, unless some happened to reside in the community). The proceedings usually took place in a saloon—which sometimes influenced the jury's decision, especially if they retired to deliberate in the liquor storeroom. Common verdicts were fines, sometimes whipping, or—for more serious offenses—banishment. Verdicts of miners' meetings were recognized by the U.S. courts, which accepted the reality that they were a logical recourse to establish order where no formal legal machinery existed.

Dolf and his employers all knew the miners' meetings would be the first basis of law in any community that sprung up as a result of the Lost Sky Pilot diggings. Dolf was intended to be their first sheriff, elected informally by the miners, just as Paul Brown had been in Juneau. Merchants' and miners' contributions, not always ungrudgingly parted with, supported the office. Undoubtedly their competitors hoped to put their man in—probably Rudy Dwan if Dolf could be disposed of first. If not, it was a certainty Dwan would remain undercover, having seen enough of Dolf's work the day he had killed Shootin' Shep.

Dolf was sipping his shot of whiskey when Goldie came on the scene to survey the crowd as most saloon owners did on and off—usually to spot any potential trouble and head it off. Dolf watched his gaze pass over the room and land on them. His face openly expressed surprise and shock.

Can't be much of a gambler if he's that easy to read, Dolf thought. For himself, he'd carefully developed a poker face for his official dealings with the public, never smiling, never altering his expression. It paid. It also got him a reputation for being cold-blooded. That didn't hurt either.

"This is an honor," Goldie greeted them. "Have one on the house, gents. I'll pour 'em myself."

Dolf switched to beer.

Seeing his attempt at pumping them fall flat, Goldie drifted away saying, "Enjoy yourselves, gents. If ya need anything special, send for me."

Seeing his chance to needle Goldie, Old John put in his oar. "There is one little thing you could do for us."

Goldie was all smiles till he heard what it was. "Just say the word," he gushed.

"Tell Rudy Dwan we invited him down for a drink."

For just an instant Goldie registered panic, then got himself under control. "Don't know the gent," he said, trying to sound casual. "Friend o' yers up with one o' my gals?"

"Not hardly," Hedley said. "I just thought he mighta taken a job with you since he's in town. He'd fit right in." He had a notion to add, "with the rest of your gorillas," but having got the needle in good, he decided to leave well enough alone.

Goldie looked blank. "Nope. Sorry. If he drops in, I'll tell him you asked for him."

"Do that," Old John suggested.

Goldie broke away as soon as he could do so politely.

"I'll bet the bastard runs upstairs like a scalded dog, provided Dwan is actually up there," Hedley said. "And Dwan won't live here anymore, maybe."

They couldn't see where Goldie went, but he didn't come back for a good ten minutes. Then he reappeared and entered a conversation with some men at the other end of the bar. Dolf noticed him checking to see if they were still there.

"I gotta go out back and see a man," Jack said. He ambled down the room, casually looking over the gambling in progress on his way. The water closets were across the back alley.

When Jack didn't come back right away, Old John said, jokingly, "He must be havin' a long talk with that fella he went to see."

A faint warning that all might not be right with Quillen began to worry Dolf.

After some ten minutes had passed, Old John said, "Are you thinkin' what I am? Maybe we'd better go see what happened to Jack. I noticed Goldie mosey out just after he left. C'mon."

He started toward the back room.

"Wait a minute," Dolf said. "I got a hunch we oughta go the other way."

Hedley nodded, following him out front.

"What's back there?" Dolf asked.

"Lotta sheds. The w.c. is across the alley from the back door."

"Let's just take a gander down both sides o' the building and see if maybe there's a reception committee back there expecting one or both of us to come out the back way. You take that side, I'll take this."

The moon was riding the horizon as it did in winter, mimicking the summer's midnight sun in reverse. An alley paralleled the Skookum, between it and the next somewhat shorter building. A pile of empty beer kegs clogged the rear of the alley, next to the saloon. Dolf couldn't be sure, but he thought he saw a head bob up among them when he first looked.

Hedley joined him. "All clear on that side," he said in a low voice.

"I think we got at least one man back among some empty beer kegs," Dolf said. "He seems all fired interested in what's out back. Maybe if we keep in the shadow right next to the building we can slip up on him."

"Why don't I decoy him. I'll check and see that Jack ain't back inside, then head out back the way they expect one of us to come. If Jack's inside by now, I'll be back and tell you in a few seconds. If I ain't, you start to injun down that way. They ain't gunnin' fer me I don't reckon, so it'll be safe to play sittin' duck. My guess is if you showed up out back, there'd be a blue whistler party waitin' fer yuh."

Dolf waited some thirty seconds; then, staying in the heavy shadow, he carefully worked his way back toward the possible ambush. He saw a figure partially rise up, probably when Old John went out the back door. He hoped it would turn out to be Rudy Dwan. As he drew closer, he could see that whoever it was had either a shotgun or a rifle; he'd have bet the former. Within only a few steps of his man, Dolf had a clear view of the water closets. Old John stepped back out of them just then. This occupied the gunman's attention so that Dolf could shove his pistol into his spine.

"Freeze," he ordered, low-voiced. Then louder, "Over here, John."

Hedley rapidly joined them.

"Take his scattergun, John, then we'll run him over an alley or two outa sight of this place and have a little confab."

They moved over beyond the adjoining building, sliding into its shadow. Dolf frisked the man and netted a six-shooter.

"You waitin' out there on anyone in particular?"

"Hell, no. I just guard the joint," the fellow lied weakly.

"The outhouse? Try again. Someone had you out there to get me."

"I don't even know you."

"Let's cut the bullshit, fellow," Hedley cut in. "We know why you were out there. What'd you gorillas do with my partner Jack Quillen? Talk up quick."

He noisily eared back the hammers on the shotgun. "In case you really don't know who we are, he's Dolf Morgette. They call me Old John Hedley. Dolf's gentle as a schoolgirl, but I'd shoot yuh jist ta see yuh kick. Now start singin'."

"Jeezuz. They never told me that. They pointed out you guys to me at the bar. Told me it'd be worth five hunnert bucks to get Morgette, but they never told me who he was. I knowed who you was. Seen yuh in town before."

"Who's they?" Dolf inquired coldly.

"I hadn't better say."

Hedley plowed the scattergun into his solar plexus. "You got three seconds. One . . . two—"

"Goldie. Goldie and the new fella. Got a funny name."

"Dwan?" Dolf said.

"Yah, that's it."

"What happened to Quillen?"

"We sapped him an' dragged him down in the cellar."

"Where's Goldie and Dwan now?"

"I dunno. Maybe down in the cellar. Inside somewhere. They planned to sweat something outa Quillen."

They were interrupted by the sound of a brief scuffle beside them further down the building toward the street.

Dolf swung his pistol in that direction to cover any approaching threat. He was astounded as he'd ever been to recognize Margaret there in the faint light. A body lay at her feet.

"What happened?" Dolf asked her, still astounded.

"He was creeping up on you with a gun in his hand. I slugged him."

"What with?"

"My father's coup stick. One end is filled with lead," she chuckled. "Us Indians aren't as ceremonial as you think."

"Let's see who you bagged," Dolf said. He turned him over. It wasn't Dwan or Goldie.

"What were you doin' out here, Margaret?" he demanded.

She thought of saying, "Rescuing you fool men." But instead she lied to save his feelings, saying, "I couldn't sleep so I took a walk. It was just lucky I stumbled on you when I did."

Dolf thought, I'll bet. He remembered how she'd shadowed him for two days at Pinebluff without his detecting her until she had wanted him to.

"What'll we do with these two?" Hedley wondered aloud. "The town ain't got a real jail. No time to run 'em down an' have Cap Magruder put 'em in irons."

"Sure there is," Dolf said. "Nobody's gonna hurt Quillen. They won't get him to talk either. You run these two down while old coup stick and I keep an eye on things here. You got any idea how to get down in the basement of the Skookum?"

"Sure. Stairway's to your right just inside the back door. Think you want to go it alone? The canal's just back here a ways. I'd just as soon club these two and put 'em in it."

"I can handle it," Dolf said. "Margaret knows how to use a

six-shooter better'n most men. She can cover my back." His inclination was to wish she was back in their room, but he had no choice under the circumstances. He smiled inwardly over his grim predicament. The man Margaret had slugged was coming around. Dolf poked him with his toe. Margaret had already appropriated the six-shooter he'd dropped.

"Get up," Dolf ordered. "And don't make any funny plays. John here's got a scattergun on yuh."

"I'll be back quick as I can and bring Cap and a couple of good men," Old John promised as he herded his two prisoners away by the back alley. "I'd hate to miss the party completely."

Dolf waited until he was sure no one was in the water closets while they crouched among the kegs where he'd bagged the first ambusher. Hoping no one would be coming out, he led the way through the back door. The hall lamp provided enough light to get them to the first landing where the basement stairs turned. From there they groped a ways until their eyes adjusted. Somewhere below another faint light outlined a long corridor ahead of them. He could smell the damp earth of the floor, mingled with a stale beer odor. As his eyes became accustomed to the gloom, he noted that the walls were of vertical board. Several doors pierced the walls on both sides of the passageway, all closed.

"We'll have to see if we can hear anything," Dolf whispered to Margaret, who was close behind him. "Or maybe see some light shining through a crack."

Quillen had just finished using the accommodation when someone entered. Before he could turn his head, he was sapped with a shot-loaded blackjack. When he came around groggily, he seemed to be hanging sideways from something. As his head cleared, he realized he was tied in a chair and had been slumped over in it. He straightened up. Two men he'd never seen before were in the room with him.

"Wakin' up," one of them said.

"Where am I?" Jack asked.

"We'll ask the questions," snapped a hulking, lantern-jawed goon with a balding, sloped head. He wore a striped seaman's shirt.

"You won't get any answers," Quillen promised.

"Wanna bet? We got ways o' makin' even the toughest ones squeal."

Quillen felt a surge of fear course through him but threw it off.

The other goon was short and squat with a slack unshaven jaw and bulging eyes. He spoke now. "We got your kid. If you want him to stay healthy, you'd better do what we say."

Quillen figured that for a bluff. His seventeen-year-old son was up at Hedley's. He'd bet there wasn't anyone in the territory—not even an Indian—could trap his son, bush-wise as he was. Nonetheless he asked, "What d'ya want me to do?"

"Draw us a nice map."

"That's what I figured. Go to hell."

With that the baldy slapped him hard both ways across his face, rocking his head violently. Quillen guessed from the strength of the blows that this one had probably boxed at some time. Even the open-handed blows had made him see stars. They also made him mad as hell.

"That's just for starters. Your kid'll get even worse if you don't loosen up."

"Bring the kid in here and I might talk," Quillen stalled. He felt sure that by now Old John and Dolf would be looking for him.

"Who wants the map?" Jack asked, stalling for more time.

"None o' your business," the whiskery one said.

"What's to stand in the road of you guys beefin' me once you get your map?"

"No need to if we get it."

"Suppose I give you a fake map? What then?"

"We're plannin' ta keep your kid all summer till we find out it ain't. If it is, he's done for."

"I can't see it," Jack said.

The pug punched him in the gut, knocking the wind out of him. He was still gasping to regain his breath when the pug hit him again. For a second or two he blacked out. He could hear the second goon say, "Take it easy. We don't want him out cold again where he can't sing."

Even when his head cleared, he was still gasping for breath. He'd never been worked over by a pro before, but it made him all the more determined.

"Now," Baldy snarled, "you gettin' ready to be reasonable?"

Quillen just glared at him. He braced for the next punch he was sure would be coming. It never did. Instead Dolf burst through the door, throwing down his six-shooter on the two goons. Quillen was startled to see Margaret come in right behind Dolf, also holding a pistol.

"Cut Jack loose," Dolf told Margaret. "And you two, over against the wall facing it."

They did as they were told. Dolf picked the lantern off the table and hung it on a nail in one of the floor joists overhead so it couldn't be kicked over if the two started a scuffle.

"Now," he ordered, "you two put your hands on the wall and back away so you're leanin' on them."

When they did, he patted them down, netting a blackjack and a six-shooter apiece. He threw these—except a six-shooter he saved for Quillen—across the room onto the dirt floor.

"Just stay there, you two."

After Quillen was loose and had gotten the feeling back in his hands, Dolf said, "We'll herd these two outside. With any luck we won't meet anyone that matters on the way. We'll put 'em in irons down on the *Idaho*. Old John already took a couple of others down there."

They were able to do this without a hitch. Old John was halfway back with Cap Magruder and two sailors packing scatterguns when they met him. Cap sent the two sailors back with the new prisoners.

"Throw 'em in the brig with the others," he told them. "I

don't know what you three are planning, but I wouldn't miss it for all the tea in China."

"Us four," Dolf corrected him. "We've got the deadliest coup stick in Alaska with us."

Old John explained the remark.

"I'll be damned," Cap snorted.

Margaret noticed that she wasn't feeling the least bit tired. She expected Dolf to send her back to the hotel and intended to protest. But he didn't, accepting her as the staunch warrior she'd proven to be.

"Whaddya reckon we should do next?" he asked Hedley.

"Take that sonofabitch Goldie out and drown him, then burn down his den of iniquity. I'm goin' in the front. I'll bring him out the back way."

He was as good as his word. In less than a minute Goldie shot out the back door ahead of him, propelled by a brawny arm holding him by the scruff of his shirt collar. A man coming in from out back eyed them all suspiciously.

"What's goin' on?" he asked.

Old John waved a six-shooter at him.

"For one thing, you're goin' ta take a short walk with us."

He herded him and Goldie around the side of the next building where Margaret had slugged the goon with her coup stick.

He said, "Cap, how about you and Quillen taking these two down to the docks. Turn this one loose. You know what to do with Goldie. Meanwhile I got one last job to do."

When the others were gone, Old John suggested, "Let's send the little lady here over to make sure the coffeepot's on at the hotel. We'll be along directly."

"I can take a hint," Margaret said. "Be sure you don't need that coup stick, though, before I leave."

Hedley actually grinned. When she was out of earshot, he said, "That's some gal." It was the highest praise; in his world, women didn't usually rate much above Chinamen.

"What're you plannin' now?" Dolf asked.

"I'm gonna burn the goddam place down just like I said."

It took Dolf five minutes to dissuade him.

"Some innocent damn fool upstairs dead drunk with some gal might get burned to death," was the clinching argument. It made sense to Old John, who'd been there in his day.

"You're right," Hedley agreed. "They'd only rebuild it again anyhow. Let's go see if Margaret has that coffee hot."

When Quillen rejoined them at the hotel, Cap Magruder was still with him.

"Didn't want to miss the next act," Cap explained. "Besides, I want to know what you want done with those gents I got ironed to the wall. Hold 'em for a miner's meeting?"

Old John Hedley thought about that while sipping his coffee.

"Hell, no. Goldie's got too many dummies around here that would fall for his line."

"Just before yuh pull outa Victoria on your way back, put 'em ashore. They can't very well complain right away about being kidnapped. Not in Canada. If Goldie comes back, it'll be at least two or three weeks from now. Maybe he'll repent over keepin' bad company. At least he'll know better'n to kidnap my partner again, eh, Quillen?"

They tried to decide how to smoke Dwan out, but decided to leave him alone and give him some rope and see what he'd do when Goldie turned up missing.

Just before he finally dozed off later that night, Dolf thought, Two mighty warriors in one family. That'll be some son. If it ain't a girl.

CHAPTER 6

IT was still dark when the small steamer *Yukon*, loaded with supplies for John Hedley's trading post, pulled out of Juneau for Dyea. Wowakan was cabled down on deck in his portable stall. The only passengers were Hedley, Quillen, and the Morgettes.

"About a ten-hour run on this tub," Hedley said for the benefit of Dolf and Margaret. "The *Yukon*'ll have to stand off for high tide to make it in to my dock once we get there. Damn tide runs twenty foot high. I got a scow to run us in so we won't have to wait for the tide—Chilkat injuns run it. Wait'll yuh see 'em. I call 'em Thunder and Lightning. Got long scraggly mustaches like them pictures of Chinamen in the old days. Strong as oxes, though. Can tote two hundred pounds over the pass and never stop to catch their breath. We'll need a bunch like 'em when you fellows go over in the spring. There's a big village of 'em up at my place. They wuz plumb hostile when I first came up here, but I got the army up from Haines to do a little target practice with a Gatling gun. O'course I hadda hang two o' the bastards myself later fer killin' my clerk."

"I already told 'em about it," Quillen said.

Hedley cackled over the recollection.

"After that Gatling gun business they never let out a peep when I swung off them two. 'Course I gave their squaws five dollars and a bolt of calico apiece. They prob'ly thought they got the best of the bargain." He laughed dryly at a sudden thought. "Maybe I shoulda asked them to pay me for services rendered."

Dolf thought, Funny thing. Back at Ft. Belton, to hear 'em tell it, Hedley was grim as sin. Here he is joking just like me or anyone else. Of course, there's no tellin' what they're sayin' about me back at Ft. Belton by now. Dolf knew what they'd said about him for years in Idaho; Mamas used to scare their

53

kids into being good by suggesting "Morgette" would come and get them otherwise. It was the way reputations were built.

Clouds loomed low overhead, ragged from turbulent air currents that didn't reach down to the water. The churning cloud blanket obscured the sky from shore to shore. Mountains hemmed in the *Yukon* on both sides, covered by almost unbroken brooding forests of spruce that crowded to the green water's edge.

A whale surfaced from the dark green depths, ran alongside for several hundred yards, then dipped gracefully beneath the water with what looked like a friendly wave of its tail. The shores appeared inviting, yet mysterious. An Indian canoe glided silently past going south, its hull dark, blending with the shadowed reflection of the spruce forest in the water.

"If we was goin' up by canoe ourselves, they might try to give us some trouble," Hedley observed. "Till we pointed a .45-90 at 'em. They're still ornery, but they 'heap savvy' Winchester medicine."

Margaret nudged Dolf and said in a very low voice, "Us injuns are bad medicine."

Dolf grinned. "How well I know it," he whispered back.

They stood close together on deck holding hands like young lovers long after the two partners had retired to the small saloon for coffee.

It was faintly light yet when the *Yukon* dropped anchor off Dyea.

"Best stay on board tonight, I guess," Hedley allowed. "My boys'll probably be out to panhandle 'kow kow,' but there's no sense in riskin' our necks out there in the scow till daylight."

As it happened, the tide was in at first light so the *Yukon* itself could use Hedley's dock.

"You show 'em up to the store an' get 'em settled, Jack," Hedley told Quillen. "I gotta stay here and see that these heathens don't break everything up or steal half of it."

The heathens were his Chilkat roustabouts, supervised by Thunder and Lightning as straw bosses.

Leading Wowakan, with Jim Too and Margaret beside him, Dolf followed Quillen up the well-beaten track to Hedley's complex of buildings. The main compound was a long low log structure with porches on both sides. In it were the store and quarters where Old John and his wife lived. Beside it was a stable and corral flanked by kennels. The dogs set up a deafening din at the sight of Jim Too.

Two detached cabins comprised the rest of the complex, one of which was for the Morgettes. The other was Quillen's, where he batched with his son when they were not up in the interior. Ropes were strung between all the buildings to guide anyone moving about at the height of a blizzard. There were only four other white men living in Dyea and about 250 Chilkat Indians over in the village.

Dolf put Wowakan in the corral, patting him affectionately on his forehead. The big horse wickered softly, then pranced and cavorted around the enclosure—happy to have even that much freedom after his long confinement.

"I know how you feel, big boy," Dolf told him. "Tomorrow I'll take you out for a run."

Quillen interrupted. "I'll show you two over to your place so you can get settled in. Afterwhile you can meet John's old woman an' my boy if he's around."

Their cabin was a neat log structure about fifteen by thirty feet with a front porch. Quillen threw open the door for Margaret to enter first.

"It's wonderful," Margaret exclaimed as she looked from room to room. It was far better than the only home they'd managed before, the one at Ft. Belton, where they really hadn't had time to get settled. By contrast, this one had been furnished straight out of the best furniture store in Portland. There'd been time enough for Baker to arrange that by mail. There were three rooms: in the front a sitting room, in the middle a kitchen, and in back the bedroom, which had a large closet. Obviously their arrival had been anticipated to the hour, since there were fires in the three stoves and the wood boxes were chuck full.

"Come look, Dolf," Margaret called happily. "It even has curtains on the windows."

She was thinking, We're home. This is where I'll have our first boy. She never thought of the child as being anything else.

"I'll leave you two for a while and go scout up my boy," Quillen said. "Take your time and relax awhile, then I'll take you over to meet John's wife, Elsie. She'd probably been here, but someone has to mind the store. She handles them ornery Chilkats better'n John—even speaks their lingo; says it's something like Sioux."

"Maybe I can pick it up too," Margaret said. "I understand Sioux and can talk it a little."

After Quillen left, she inspected the entire house.

"It even has two kitchen cupboards!" she exclaimed. "And they both have a flour sifter, and they're full of groceries, too."

Dolf was happy watching her. He, too, was thinking that this was where their first child would be born. That there were no doctors for miles didn't worry either of them. Dolf's mother had never had a doctor for any of her children. Margaret's people didn't know the meaning of one; Elsie's hadn't either. Indians had midwives. Any Indian woman knew how to handle that task.

Dolf tried the bed, finding it exceptionally comfortable. He stretched out on it, placing his hands behind his head, fingers laced. Jim Too flopped comfortably on the floor beside him in what was to become his favorite spot.

"Well, Maggie, I guess we're home."

She came and snuggled beside him, looking into his eyes, her own large and dark. "Yes, we're home. And I love it." Impulsively, she planted a warm generous kiss on his lips. "And I love you, Dolf. Don't ever leave me."

He looked at her with a perplexed frown. "What a funny thing to say. Why would I leave you?"

But a twinge of guilt tugged at his conscience, for her remark reminded him of Victoria's letter, which he still hadn't been able to throw away. He wondered if she'd seen him rereading it and carefully hiding it, if perhaps she'd guessed what it was or even gone through his papers when he was out. Women, he knew, were capable of such things. He remembered his innocent trust of Theodora, his first wife, of whom he'd been able to suspect no evil. He drove these thoughts from his mind, too happy with the present to permit them to mar his contentment. But Margaret remained quiet and pensive beside him, not answering his question. He didn't press her for one.

Quillen brought his son over that first day. "This is Avery; everyone calls him Ave," he introduced the big, bashful kid.

Dolf, sensing the boy's unease, grabbed his hand and pumped it. "Call me Dolf. And this is Margaret, but I reckon she'll let you call her Maggie."

Ave gulped shyly.

"Howdy, ma'am. Howdy, Mr. Morgette—I mean Dolf." He flushed over his possible impoliteness.

Both the Morgettes had been surprised at their first sight of Ave. He almost had to stoop to get through the door. Dolf guessed he was at least six foot six. Strong, too, I'd bet, he thought.

"You two are our first real guests," Margaret said. "I'm fixing coffee, and we were going to have warm bread and jelly. Won't you two have some with us?"

Margaret wasn't much older than Ave in years, but she knew the way to a growing boy's heart, whether he was Indian or white. That broke the ice. They all lounged around the big oak table with its checked oilcloth cover, stuffing themselves on the delicious fresh bread. The kitchen was cosy from the range's radiant warmth.

"I seen yer hoss, Dolf," Ave finally managed to get out. He grinned shyly. "He let me touch him, though he was mighty leery o' me at first. I don't remember seein' many real hosses, just pictures mostly, but that's the best one I ever saw. He's sure big."

Dolf had to smile. "You're one o' the few. I'm gonna have to talk to that animal. Up till now, he won't let anyone but me and Maggie get friendly with him."

"Took me most a half hour," Ave admitted. "I fed him a potato."

Dolf was really surprised at that. He couldn't even get Wowakan to touch oats or corn when he'd first got him. Indian horses didn't know that kind of food. At first he'd sniffed, snorted in alarm, and shied away. Only after many patient attempts had Dolf been able to teach him that it was good.

"Did he take it out of your hand?"

"Yup."

"I *am* amazed, Ave." He'd caught himself almost saying "kid" but figured it might embarrass a kid who was six foot six.

That day was the start of a hero-worshipping friendship on Ave's part. As for Dolf, he could see his own son, Junior, in Quillen's quiet, capable boy, and he liked having him around. The two boys were about the same age—Junior slightly older but not as tall. A happy thought occurred to Dolf, one he was sure would please the big "kid."

"If Wowakan likes yuh, he may let you ride him. If he will, you can give him some regular exercise. He can run like the wind."

"Wowakan." Ave caressed the word. "I like his name."

As they were leaving, Quillen ducked back in. "Dolf, you're a marvel. That kid ain't talked that much to anybody but me in his whole life."

Dolf looked surprised. "Well, I'm proud to hear it. I like him. He's a great kid. And we will see if Wowakan'll let him ride."

The next morning Dolf saddled the big horse to ride him himself, at least to get the edge off of him. Wowakan was so eager he was hard to mount.

"Steady, idjit," Dolf chided him. He had to crowd the horse's rear end to the corral fence, then quickly get a foot in the stirrup, mounting on the fly as Wowakan practically leaped into a run at one bound. Someone not born to the saddle would have been left sprawling on the frozen ground. Their first half mile was a runaway, Dolf enjoying it as much as the horse did. After that he reined him down to a ground-eating lope. With the wind rushing past, he was almost unsure that he heard the bullet buzz past till the rifle's distant report reached them. Not wanting to risk his horse, he touched spurs to him and pounded out of range. No second shot sounded.

He tethered Wowakan behind a rise densely crowned with willows, then cautiously worked up to where he could survey his back trail. He'd expected to see no one and wasn't disappointed. He circled to ride the tidal flats since the shot had come from over in the fringe of brush growing just above high tide. Cautiously, he rode along the muddy margin between brush and beach, alert for any threatening movement, but also watching for tracks. He wondered if Dwan had already followed him. Or was it someone else? The other side could certainly have hired almost anyone for a job like that—even one of the surly Chilkats. He sure intended to find out if he could. The best way he could figure to make inquiries about any strangers in the vicinity was through Hedley and his two faithful Chilkats. He also made a note to strap his .45-90 on the saddle whenever he rode from then on.

"I'll send Thunder 'n' Lightnin' up there to check for sign," said Hedley when informed of the ambush attempt. "Also have 'em sound out the village for any information. If a greenhorn like Dwan is up here, we'll smoke him out unless he's got some injun sidekicks to show him how to hide out an' siwash it in the bush. That is a possibility. All these injun'll do anything for a price—the Chilkats, Hoonahs, even the Sticks over in the

Yukon. I don't trust any of 'em except my two, and I don't let my guard down around them. Don't you either."

Efforts to discover who may have tried to potshoot Dolf netted nothing. "The bastards musta hired someone who lives around here," Hedley guessed. "Probably some o' the Chilkats over in the village. The whites up here are all farmers—ain't the type fer that kinda work. They all work for me. Typical Honyackers I brought from Montana."

"You'll have ta keep yer eyes open from now on," added Quillen. "I didn't expect they'd start in again till we went over the other side next spring. They're gonna be a tougher proposition than I figured."

Quillen undertook Dolf's instruction in the fine points of snowshoeing and mushing a dog team. Dolf's first problem with the long Indian snowshoes was that he kept getting the fronts stuck in the snow, then falling face forward.

Quillen laughed the first time. "Don't feel silly. You should see me on a horse. In a coupla weeks I'll have you runnin' on those things."

He gave a demonstration, lifting the toes high, with a slightly spread-legged gate. He could go surprisingly fast. Dolf practiced, and as the days passed the spills came less frequently. Jack Quillen proved a prophet. In under two weeks, Dolf was able to do a passable job of running on snowshoes. All this time they were also working the sled teams, one behind on the gee pole to guide it and keep it from tipping, the other ahead to break trail. At first it had been numbingly exhausting for Dolf, who kept going until it seemed the next icy breath would burn out his lungs or choke him. But he wasn't a quitter. Soon he began to harden his body to it and develop his wind.

On these initial lessons, they hadn't brought along Jim Too. Quillen knew it would completely shatter team discipline as the whole team would chase him and try to fight with him.

Besides, Jack wanted to get the team used to Dolf and give him a chance to establish the moral domination where they recognized that he was absolute boss. Jack noticed that Dolf had a remarkable way of making animals mind him; he didn't even have to beat a single animal.

"I never seen the like o' you, Dolf," Quillen commented. "Any man I ever seen work dogs woulda had to club a couple of 'em at least to git where he could work 'em the way you do. How d'ya do it?"

"I'm part dog, I guess," Dolf allowed.

"If you was part dog, they'da et you up before now. More like part wolf, I'd guess—or grizzly bear. Whatever it is, them dogs can sense it."

The part about what the fierce huskies would do to a dog was luckily avoided when Jim Too was allowed to join them. Quillen had an idea how to simplify things. "The toughest one o' them dogs in either team is Scuffy; an' the biggest. If you got no objections, let's bring him out an' let the two o' 'em get acquainted the hard way."

Dolf thought about that. Jim Too was pretty well past the puppy stage, probably at least fifteen months old. He wasn't as seasoned as he would be at three or four, but he'd shown what he could do to Goldie's hefty malamute. Scuffy was no bigger, and maybe no tougher than Goldie's dog had been.

"Why not," Dolf agreed. "That's the way Pa taught us boys to handle ourselves. Go ahead and turn 'em loose."

Scuffy, as they expected, tore out like he intended to take Jim Too apart. Then a strange ritual transpired. He saw Jim Too simply standing his ground, looking at him warily. Scuffy stopped his headlong attack, then slowly—stiff-legged with his hackles standing up in a high ruff—approached and touched noses with Dolf's dog. After a long sniff, he tentatively wagged his tail and walked stiffly around Jim Too, who also wagged his tail a bit. Finally they sniffed each other, then they crouched down like puppies inviting a romp. In another instant they were tearing around in a circle like long-lost littermates. Finally they bounded shoulder to shoulder into the brush, running heedlessly into one another every other leap.

Quillen and Dolf exchanged amazed looks.

Jack exploded, "Well I'll be go to hell! Ain't that the damndest thing yuh ever saw?"

When the two dogs returned, both out of breath, Scuffy led his new-found friend down the line of dog pens as if he were introducing him to each occupant. On later occasions, Jim Too nonetheless had to introduce each of the others to the medicine he'd administered to Goldie's dog, but when he did, Scuffy never allowed any of the others to gang up on him.

Trouble was the furthest thing from Dolf's mind as he was stabling his big horse for the night. Dark was already falling, so he had the lantern lit in the barn. He stooped to feel a roughened spot on one of Wowakan's fetlocks where he thought perhaps the crusty snow had cut him. As he did, a hatchet thunked wickedly into the nearby post supporting the stall, burying itself deep in the wood.

The noise puzzled him till he glanced around to see what had caused it. Then he quickly spun, shucking out a pistol, scanning the gloom. The barn door slammed, and running footsteps were audible in the crusty snow. He slipped to the door, cautiously looking out. A shadowy figure disappeared, running full tilt around the corner of the store building. Dolf quickly ran after it. As he mounted the porch, Ave was just coming out the door. He looked startled to see Dolf, pistol in hand.

"Did you see anyone run up here just now?" Dolf asked.

Ave looked blank for a moment. "Only Thunder. He came in just before I came out."

"Where'd he go?"

"Headed in the back somewhere."

"C'mon," Dolf said. "I want someone who can talk his lingo."

Inside, Hedley looked as surprised as Ave to see Dolf with a gun in his hand.

"What's up?" he inquired.

"Your boy Thunder just threw a hatchet at me in the barn. I saw him run up on the porch outside, and Ave saw him come in just now. If I hadn't stooped down when I did, I'd be laying out there with a hand axe in my head."

Hedley had also seen Thunder come in and go to the storeroom.

"Thunder!" Hedley roared. "Git the hell out here."

Slowly, Thunder emerged from the back room, trying to appear innocent, but with guilt written all over him when he said, "Ya, boss. Wat you want?"

Old John got his story out of him fast. They were more afraid of Hedley than of the big brown bears that occasionally lunched on humans out in the bush.

"Hoonah Charlie made me do, boss. He say bad medicine," Thunder explained, pointing at Dolf. "Make all inchen die."

Hedley got a more rational story from him in his own tongue. Hoonah Charlie had convinced the Chilkats that Dolf was bad medicine, possessed of the evil spirits that caused the measles, scarlet fever, and whooping cough—which had killed off the tribes like flies in some past seasons. Hoonah Charlie told them Dolf was going to go over to the Yukon in the spring. All the Indians that provided furs to the Chilkats would die if the Chilkats themselves didn't die first. It was obvious then that Dolf had to be killed. Thunder didn't want to do it because he knew it would make Old John mad, but for the sake of his people he had to.

"Why, you simple-minded dunce!" John roared at him. "Don't you know somebody hired Hoonah Charlie to tell you that big lie?"

Thunder hung his head. "Uh uh. Thunder not know dat," he said contritely.

"Jeezus!"

John explained to Dolf why Thunder had tried to kill him.

Dolf said, "Ask him if he took that shot at me."

Hedley complied. "He did that, too."

"Well," Dolf said. "That explains the single shot. I thought that thing sounded like an old muzzle loader."

"Yuh know what this adds up to," Hedley said. "Every damn injun in creation is lookin' fer a try at yuh. Be the same over the other side come spring. I can probably convince our tribe here that Hoonah Charlie told a lie. They understand lies, being so good at 'em themselves. It'll figure to them especially that somebody lied for money. But it won't be so easy over in the Yukon in the spring. You can bet that Hoonah Charlie will be over there peddling his story ahead of you all the way. It don't take a genius to figure out who paid Hoonah Charlie either."

"Dwan," Dolf said.

"And company," Hedley added. "I heared Goldie finally got back to his old stand. I may go down and burn him out yet, just fer the hell of it. You stick close by fer a couple of days till I get a chance to spike that story. I'm bettin' Dwan ain't the type to hang around here in the bush; he'll depend on them injuns. Once I get it straightened out, yuh can probably breathe easy till spring."

Maybe, Dolf thought.

CHAPTER 7

ALTHOUGH Dolf's conscience had forbidden his answering Victoria Wheat's letter, there were equal ties of love dictating that he write to his family. The complication in writing home now would be that it might disclose his whereabouts to authorities interested in extraditing him to Canada over the recent fizzled attempt to rescue Henri Lemoine. No overt effort had been initiated by the Canadians, Ira Baker had written in a letter to Hedley, but suspicion was strong that they were aware Dolf had disappeared and were merely waiting for the U.S. authorities to discover his whereabouts first.

Complications were circumvented by John Hedley who, through an intermediary, had opened correspondence with Dolf's oldest and staunchest friend at Pinebluff, Doc Hennessey. Dolf sent Doc a package of letters, one each to his son Dolf Jr., his daughter Amy, his brother Matt, and his curmudgeon of a grandmother, Mum, who was now ranching with Matt. Finally he wrote a long letter to Doc himself, explaining his reasons for leaving, as well as subsequent events and his current situation—even his unhappy state of mind.

Writing these letters lifted a burden from Dolf's mind. He felt sure he had hurt them all by running away when he had, but the disappointment over losing Victoria Wheat at that time had been more than he could face on top of his crushing years in prison.

Despite his affinity for violence when it was thrust upon him, Dolf possessed a profound ability to love, coupled with a great romantic's vulnerability to it. To him, love was much more than the animal thing he realized it was for many—perhaps most—men. He was totally incapable of the casual "love for sale" liaisons that his associates on the frontier were addicted to. He accepted them in others with amiable toleration, but was nonetheless completely incapable of understanding them. His attitude toward women, even the coarse women he'd necessarily encountered as a lawman, was one of protectiveness and worshipful pity, especially for those laid low by misfortune in a world that greatly favored men.

It was this tender facet of his nature that cemented his devotion to Margaret. He would never forsake her despite the perverse fate that had deceived him into his great responsibility to her. He realized he could never betray her trust. She loved him; that he knew. That was enough to bind him to her forever.

Dolf's days consisted of continuing his training for the ordeal ahead which might encompass a several year commitment. He was becoming as adept at dogsledding as he was at horsemanship. In this manner Dolf's days passed blandly with no further attempts on his life. Thunder actually seemed to be pathetically protective of him since coming to realize he'd been deceived into trying to kill him.

The nights were idyllic. He and Margaret often took walks, the moonlight silvering their path among the bushes and the trees sparkling like diamonds with frost. Sometimes the Northern lights would enchant their world, rippling across the sky from horizon to horizon or painting vast looping swirls overhead in rainbow colors, all accompanied by a subdued sibilance, a hushed whisper that not all people could hear.

Margaret had no apprehension over her impending first delivery, unlike many women who had a secret dread of what they knew would be inevitably painful, perhaps deadly.

"Nothing is more natural," she scoffed.

One morning they were surprised, then amused, by an unexpected visitor. They'd heard muffled noises out front before rising, but had assumed it was some of the regular trading-post retinue going about hauling wood or doing some other chore. When Dolf got up to stoke the stoves—as he always did before allowing Margaret to get out of bed—he glanced out the window. In the dim early light, he was startled

to see a new ungainly structure, apparently a tattered tent, standing a few feet from the porch. He opened the door to investigate more closely and found a huddled figure squatted on the porch.

"Who are you?" he inquired.

A muffled voice from somewhere inside the bundlesome fur parka said, "Me Mama Borealis. Elsie send. Me fix baby, they come."

The notion penetrated Dolf's still-sleepy mind that this must be the midwife Elsie had promised. He wasn't overly assured by the first appearance. He stepped back inside.

"Hey, Maggie, come see this," he called.

His tone of voice brought her out promptly in nightgown and bare feet. He again went out on the porch. Mama Borealis had risen to her feet. Margaret eyed her from the door.

"This is Mama Borealis, Maggie. I think she's the midwife Elsie mentioned."

"Yah," Mama said, pointing a finger at her chest. "All same midwife."

Margaret impulsively took her hand and pulled her toward the warmth of the cabin.

"Come on in, Mama. You must be frozen. How long have you been out there in the cold?"

"Only leetle while. Mama used to."

"Here, sit down. We'll have kow kow in a little while."

They left her contentedly seated on the horsehair sofa, looking around with great interest at everything. Back in the bedroom, Dolf sighed, "She's probably crawling with lice."

"I don't think so," Maggie disagreed. "They freeze them out in the winter. Even if she is, we've got insect powder. We can't keep the poor good-hearted thing out in the cold. She's come to help."

"But it's at least ten days yet, isn't it?" Dolf grumbled.

"I can use the help," Margaret said.

So Mama Borealis stayed for breakfast and was to stay much longer, it appeared, whether Dolf was happy about it or not.

Margaret took to her instantly. She'd been picking up their language and could talk to her in a little of Chilkat; Mama could manage pidgin English pretty well. That first morning over coffee (which Mama took with half sugar when she discovered it was all right), Margaret got the short, simple story of her recent tragedy.

Mama said stoically, "Man die. All kid die. Mama heap cry." But there were suppressed tears in her voice. It seemed that her entire immediate family had succumbed to an epidemic of measles and now she was entirely alone.

To Dolf's pretended disgust, Margaret fixed a cot in their parlor and it became Mama's quarters. After she got her furs off, they could see that she wasn't really old—perhaps thirty. She was also rather nice-looking after Margaret persuaded her to clean up a little. To his perplexed amusement, Dolf found himself liking her. They discovered that Old John had originally dubbed her Mama Borealis because when he'd first seen her, she was raggedly garbed in a motley assortment of multicolored cast-off clothing.

Margaret tactfully but purposefully set about teaching Mama to keep a white man's house. She was smart and willing. After a couple of days, she was working away while contentedly humming to herself. Dolf was deeply touched to see her lovingly pat Margaret's head and say, tears in her eyes, "Maggie, I love you. I be *your* mama now. You my big new baby." Margaret impulsively embraced her, tears quickly coming to her own eyes.

I'll be damned, Dolf thought. Don't that beat a hog flyin'? But he felt a little lump in his own throat. He'd had so little love in his own tortured, lonely life that the evidence of true devotion always affected him deeply.

Mama had become almost a fixture by the time Margaret's labor pains started. She and Dolf were in bed, he sound asleep, when her first contraction came. She had been dozing restlessly. She smiled even though it hurt. She knew that with a first child it might be another twelve hours or more. There was no need to arouse Dolf. It was almost a half hour before she felt the second one. She tried to catch a little sleep between the spasms. By morning they were spaced closer together, making her gasp when they were sharpest. Dolf turned restlessly, beginning to wake up. She hoped her uncomfortable stirring hadn't roused him. When she knew he was fully awake, she said, "I'm having labor pains."

He rolled over quickly. "Did they just start?"

She didn't answer immediately, grasped by another pain.

"Uh huh," she said. "In the middle of the night."

He jumped up quickly, pulling on his trousers. "Why the hell didn't you wake me up?"

She smiled in the early dawn light, looking to him more beautiful than ever. "I knew it would be hours yet. There wasn't anything anyone could do. Still isn't. It probably won't be till dark when our boy finally comes."

He frowned impatiently. "I could have held you, at least. I'll tell Mama. Then I'm gonna get Elsie. She can help."

Like most men, he didn't have the faintest idea what to do. When she let out a little involuntary moan at the latest spasm, he grabbed her hand, then dropped it and galloped out to get Mama Borealis.

Mama came and placed her cool hand on Margaret's forehead; a sense of well-being pervaded Margaret.

"My baby Maggie gon' be okay," Mama assured her. "Tomorrow be a nice boy—hurt feel good then." She held Margaret's hand.

Elsie arrived right behind Dolf. She was in the bedroom for some time. Dolf, drinking coffee at the kitchen table, could hear their voices. Once he heard Margaret moan softly. He tensed inwardly, hurting with her.

He wished Doc were here now. Doc Hennessey had a reputation among the women in northern Idaho and even across the Bitterroots in Montana as the best baby doctor in creation.

Lord knew he'd delivered hundreds of them and lost damn few.

What the hell am I fretting about? Dolf thought to himself. He tried to be calm, but he knew—although he didn't want to admit it—what the trouble was. His sixth sense that had warned him of danger to himself so often and so surely in the past was sending him a premonition that everything was not going to be all right. Despite his attempt at reassuring himself, he couldn't avert the hateful thought, What will I do if she dies? It was then that he was absolutely sure for the first time that he loved his little wildflower Maggie, and no one else.

It didn't help when Jim Too started to howl dolefully whenever Margaret had one of the sharp pains and cried out. Dolf desperately tried to shrug off the memory of old granny tales he'd never really believed about dogs knowing when death will visit. He took Jim Too out and secured him at the kennels, but it didn't stop his howling. Dolf hoped Maggie didn't notice, or at least that she hadn't heard of the old superstition.

Word had got around. In a while Jack Quillen and his son dropped in for some coffee. Ave looked scared, as though he wanted to run away whenever he heard Margaret's little cries of agony. They tried to make small talk and pretend the life-or-death struggle wasn't there just behind them, but they made a poor job of it. They soon left.

"If you need anything, let me know," Jack said as they went out the door.

Elsie came out in a while and sat down with Dolf, knowing a husband's need of some reassurance at such a time. She squeezed Dolf's hand. "She's sort of narrow, and I'm afraid she's having a bad time of it, but there's no need to worry. The first one is always like that. She's strong and healthy." Elsie left then, saying, "I'll be back in a while and stay till it comes. Keep the stoves good and hot. I'm going to bring over some extra lamps since it might come after dark. We'll need all the light we can get."

Dolf's ordeal was mild compared to Margaret's, and of a wholly different kind. She was thinking, not always coherently, I didn't know. I just didn't know. I wonder if something's wrong?

It was then she felt her first fear. "I want Dolf," she told Mama. He looked scared when he came into the room. Her mood changed at once to one of wanting to reassure *him*. She took the big hand he extended to her and squeezed it, trying to smile, but one of the monstrous spasms grasped her and she cried out. After it passed, she smiled weakly. "I'll be all right," she said. "Kiss me." He did as she asked, as near to panic as he'd ever been in his life.

"You're gonna be just fine, honey," he managed to say in a convincing tone. "I wish I could have it for you."

She vaguely thought, Men have probably said that since the dawn of time. Nonetheless, hearing it comforted her. Counterbalancing this was her awareness of Jim Too's howling. Contrary to Dolf's hope, she was fully aware of the superstition that dogs possessed insight regarding the imminent death of those they loved. In her half-Indian system of beliefs, she didn't know whether it was a superstition—as she knew most whites held it to be—or a grim fact.

After he left, Mama again sat beside her, holding her hand. She began to sweat, and Mama periodically wiped off her face. Sometime in the afternoon, Mama pulled down the bed-covers and examined her closely. Margaret tried to read the midwife's face, but if she was concerned, she was too expert at the business to mirror it to the patient. Before dark Elsie came over to stay.

"When the pains come, bear down with them," Elsie said.

"I-I-I'll try," Margaret gasped. "Oo it hurts so."

Dolf could easily hear this, even out in the parlor where Old John and Quillen had joined him for moral support.

"I guess it's a hard case," said Old John. "Listened to plenty of 'em with my first wife, but I'm bettin' it won't be long."

He said it so matter-of-factly that Dolf felt relieved of his anxiety for a little while. The next scream from the bedroom put a quick end to his temporary feeling of confidence.

Elsie came out briefly and said, "We've got to turn the baby. It's crosswise, Mama says."

Dolf was speechless; he had no idea what that meant. Old John was far from speechless. "What the hell does that mean?"

Elsie gave him an exasperated look. "It means Mama's got to turn it. That's what she's tryin' to do now. We need a couple of you big boobies to hold Margaret. Not you, Dolf—you'd probably faint. You two come on and be quick about it."

Dolf had never felt so hopeless or so resigned; he was teetering on the border of panic. He wasn't much given to praying, but he was doing it now. One theme kept running through his head: Please, God, let her live.

The struggle went on, seemingly endless, the screams becoming more subdued. Dolf knew the worst was happening when Mama herself came out. She had huge tears in her eyes. "Mama can't do. You come," she said.

He felt as he had when Wild Jim Ott had shot him almost in his heart. He could barely walk. As he tried to compose himself, the front door burst open. He thought he must be losing his mind.

"What the hell's goin' on in this shebang?"

"Doc!" Dolf managed to say. "Is that really you? Margaret's in there dying!"

"I'll be goddamned if that's so!" Doc snapped. "Bring them things!" he shouted.

Thunder and Lightning came in, packing Doc's big medicine chest. Without waiting, Doc headed for the bedroom. Dolf followed. The sight of Margaret almost undid him. She was as white as a sheet, her hair straggled and damp, her body in a grotesque position.

"Is she dead?" Dolf asked.

"Not by a damn sight!" Doc snapped. "Get that dresser with them lamps closer to the bed. I'm gonna need light."

With a few deft movements, he opened the chest the two

Chilkats had brought in. "You men get the hell outa here. Especially you, Dolf. If ya got any whiskey, take about a water glass of it. Them's Doctor's orders."

Dolf managed to get back as far as the kitchen table and collapse limply in a chair. Yet he could feel hope rising in him. He had absolute faith that if anyone on earth could save Maggie now, it would be Doc Hennessey.

Old John knew where Dolf kept the prescription Doc had ordered. He poured three of them and passed one each to Dolf and Jack. "We can all use one," he said.

The next half hour passed for Dolf like a bad dream. It seemed like forever before he heard the healthy birth yell of their baby. He came as near then to simply passing out from relief as he ever had in his life.

Old John prescribed another round of the same. In a while Doc himself came out, weary and disheveled, but looking happy.

"It's a boy," he announced. "A big one none the worse fer wear. Can't say the same for his maw. I hadda do a cesarean delivery. She's all sewed up and barrin' complications should be as good as new in a few weeks."

He washed up, took a dose of his own prescription, winked at Dolf, then returned to the bedroom whistling. He let Dolf come in for a little while to get a peek at his son. Dolf also stooped and kissed his still-unconscious wife. She looked a lot better, with healthy color returning to her face.

Dolf had never been happier in his life. He was not given to emotion, but just then he thought he was going to break down and cry. Recognizing the symptoms, Old John suggested, "Let's us three girls here all step out and have a cigar on Dolf. I got a fresh bunch over at my place."

Over at the store they encountered Thunder. Old John asked him where Doc had materialized from.

"Come in canoe in dark with buncha dem damn Hoonah paddle 'im like hell. Doc fella say him have big hunch. Come quick."

Dolf then told the others who Doc was.

"An act of God," Jack said.

"I'll smoke to that," Old John agreed. "Here." He handed Thunder a cigar. "And take one over to Lightning."

Dolf didn't sleep a wink, sitting most of the night at the kitchen table. Occasionally Doc, who spent most of the night at the bedside in a chair, joined him for some coffee.

"How's she doin'?" Dolf asked each time.

"Fine as wine," Doc reassured him. "Sleepin' peaceful. She even woke up the last time the kid nursed and smiled at me."

"Did she say anything?"

Doc laughed. "You won't believe it, but she said, 'I knew you'd come in time,' then dropped off to sleep. Maybe she did. Indians have lots of ways about 'em we don't understand. Remember how Strong Bull saved you with his dried ants and hocuspocus?"

Dolf remembered all right. Strong Bull was a medicine man in Margaret's tribe. She had brought him to save Dolf's life.

Mama Borealis took to following Doc around watching him with worshipful eyes. At first when he'd cut the incision in Margaret, she'd thought he was killing her. Elsie had had to restrain her and hastily explain. After Mama realized that he'd saved her two new babies and that his name was Doc, she dubbed him Skookum Doc. Skookum was a word with a multitude of meanings. In this case it undoubtedly meant "one damn big fine sumbitch of a medicine man."

When Doc found that out, he said, "Damned if I ain't at that."

CHAPTER 8

MARGARET was on the mend, even more quickly than Skookum Doc had guessed. Mama Borealis was so ecstatic over the fact that Margaret could nurse the new boy herself that Doc observed wryly, "We may have to put rocks in her mukluks to hold her down." (A mukluk, as Doc had just recently learned, was the native high-topped fur boot.)

The question of naming this noisy, red-faced child was high on the Morgette agenda. Dolf spent hours, whenever he could, sitting beside the bed talking with Margaret or mutely holding her hand. When she'd drop off to sleep, as she did quite often the first few days after her ordeal, he'd remain and simply watch her. They had a regular baby cradle, but Margaret wanted her boy with her as much as possible.

Looking at Dolf shyly one day, she said, "I've been thinking, honey—I'd like to name our son after my father. How does Henry sound to you?"

He had no hesitation since the same thought had been on his mind. But he'd wanted *her* to select the name.

"I thought we should pick his middle name after Doc," she went on. "He saved both of us. What is Doc's first name?"

"Skookum," Dolf said gravely.

Margaret laughed. "Silly, I mean his real name."

Dolf had simply called him Doc for so many years that he had to think about it. "John," he said. "As a matter of fact, John Henry, so in a way we've already named the kid for Doc, too."

"How about calling him Henry Doc?" Margaret suggested, poker-faced, with one of her impish flashes of humor.

"How about Henry D.? I don't have a middle name, just an initial R., after my grandad. If an initial is good enough for his paw, it oughta suit the kid."

He reached down and picked him up, carefully cradling

him in his arms. His son regarded him from solemn, slightly unfocused, unwinking eyes. "How about it, son, will Henry D. suit you okay?"

The solemn regard continued. "He ain't talkin'," Dolf said, "so I guess he doesn't have any serious objections." Then the baby yawned. "In fact, he's just about to go to sleep."

Dolf sat contentedly cradling his sleeping son in his arms, rocking him gently, oblivious to the rest of the world as he watched the peaceful little face that was poked out of the small blanket. Margaret watched them both with infinite tenderness. She was so happy to be alive still and to have a son — and a "mighty warrior," too, who was so loving beneath the taciturn protective mask he usually displayed to the world.

Jim Too had been allowed to come back in and occupy his favorite bedside roosting spot. When Dolf first showed him young Henry D., the dog immediately wagged his tail and tried to lick the baby's face. Dolf was glad to see this, knowing as he did that dogs were sometimes jealous of new babies. When Dolf returned Henry to Margaret's arms Jim Too sat up alertly at the edge of the bed watching. From that moment on, Henry was Jim Too's adopted responsibility.

"We've got another nurse, I guess," Dolf observed. It was already obvious that Mama Borealis was going to be a permanent member of the family. She hadn't returned to the village, and neither Dolf nor Margaret had the slightest desire to suggest that she ought to. In fact, they both objected when Elsie Hedley brought the subject up with them, wondering if she should save them the possible embarrassment of asking Mama to leave.

Dolf grinned as he told Elsie, "We've talked it over. We've adopted her — and she's adopted us."

"Good," Elsie said. "Maggie'll have someone to stay here with her when you're across in the Yukon next summer."

"She ain't gonna be here," Dolf said.

"You aren't sending her outside, I hope."

"Nope. She's comin' with me. So's Mama."

Elsie frowned for a moment. Then, after thinking it over, she said, "That's what I'd do, too, if I were her."

As spring approached, Old John had several strategy sessions with Dolf and Jack Quillen. When he found out that Doc planned to go with Dolf over into the Yukon country, he included him in their meetings without question. Doc and Old John had definitely hit it off from the beginning. In the first place, though he seldom showed his feelings, Old John loved Margaret as though she were his own daughter, and Doc had saved Margaret's life. But beyond that he recognized a kindred spirit in Doc—a man who, despite his humanitarian calling and manner of practicing it, recognized that the world could sometimes be improved by bumping someone off who needed it and, moreover, had no compunction about doing it summarily when the occasion demanded. Doc had been particularly titillated over the story of Old John's hanging the two Indians under the noses of a bunch of goggle-eyed tenderfeet.

"I wish I'd seen it," Doc chortled.

"Mebbe we'll need to do it to a couple more before spring," Old John allowed, hopefully.

"I could send the cadavers back to my alma mater," Doc said. "Packed in million-year-old ice off the glacier back there. My old anatomy prof. would probably use the ice to cool a case of beer or two while it lasted."

The serious business of their meetings had to do with coordinating activities that would start in earnest when the ice broke up in the chain of lakes leading to the Yukon. Water travel was the key to moving any sizable load of supplies into the interior, and Chilkoot Pass was the entrance to the country inside. Until recently, the Chilkats had jealously barred it to protect their fur monopoly with the interior tribes. Then it had dawned on them that the business of packing supplies over the pass for whites could be almost equally lucrative. And the potential of the U.S. gunboats' armament had not been lost on them either after a few displays of power. The gunboat commanders had forcefully made the point that if whites couldn't use the pass, Indians couldn't use the water. This made good sense to the Chilkats, particularly since the whites who wanted to use the pass weren't competing fur traders; they were almost all prospectors. Gold had no meaning to the Indians yet; in fact, it never would, except to a few "progressives."

"We got two ends of this deal to mesh," Old John explained. "The ice goes out of Lake Bennett sometime maybe as late as June. You fellers'll be there way before then. I got some experienced men comin' in to whipsaw out some lumber and build your boats. Some of 'em are old white-water men and will go down the river with the boats. I don't think Brown and Shadley's crowd'll bother that end of it, because they know you've got to lead them to where the Lost Sky Pilot is. They'll be in there somewhere buildin' boats themselves. Let 'em. The only one'll have to watch out every minute is Dolf here. We already know they'd like to see him on a slab, and it doesn't make any difference to their plans when.

"With you, Jack," he pointed his cigar at Quillen, "you'll only have to watch out after you stake your claims. They'll try to jump 'em. That'd be easier if you was to have an accident. What they haven't figured is our ace in the hole. We're after the trade mostly, not the gold. I aim to have you tell every prospector you meet where you're goin' and have 'em tag along. Must be two hundred of 'em winterin' inside. There's that many in Juneau that I'll get the word to, and we'll attract a lot more from all over the world as soon as I spread the word."

Quillen had already known this was the plan. It made sense to Dolf, too. If the miners' meeting was to be the basis of law and order—which was where he figured in the picture—the more miners the better; they probably wouldn't become Rudy Dwan's pawns. Dolf's main concern for the time being was staying alive and helping Maggie regain her strength. As for taking a baby on the long trip, well, the Indians did it all the time, didn't they? He was counting on Maggie's Indian training to cope with whatever minor problems came up in traveling with a baby. Doc's coming along set his mind at rest regarding possible medical emergencies.

"The other end of the deal is St. Michael," Old John explained. "I'm handlin' that myself. The ice'll be out up that way maybe earlier than in Lake Bennett. At least no later. My crews shoulda been layin' the hulls of two riverboats during the winter an' puttin' in most of the machinery. About all we'll have to do is launch 'em and load 'em. It's between seven and eight hundred miles to where you're headed. If you leave the middle o' June, you could run day and night, but we ain't in a big rush because it'll take me a lot longer comin' up from St. Michael. My best guess is about seventeen hundred miles or so from St. Michael to where you'll meet me. Figure we can average six miles an hour upstream with high water, and figure four hours a day takin' on wood. That figures out to a hundred and twenty miles a day at best. It's gonna take around fifteen days comin' up. Figure ten days for you comin' down, Jack. Either one of us could be later, but I don't figure on either of us bein' earlier. If we both left the middle of June, you have five days on me to cut over the ridge and stake them claims, then get back down by way of the river and meet me. If the Sky Pilot River or whatever we decide to call it will carry my boats, I aim to come up it to meet yuh. You can bet Brown and Shadley's boats'll be taggin' along behind me. If I can shake 'em about there and pull up toward your diggins, they'll be lost for a week most likely, lookin' fer me. Now Jack, I'll need you to send one boat downstream to meet me so I know where the hell I'm goin' for sure. Or maybe I can hire a pilot away from the A.C. Co. I wouldn't have to tell 'im exactly what I'm headed for till we're almost there."

"I can save maybe a hundred miles hoofin' it over the ridge," said Quillen. "Me 'n' Dolf an' my boy could go in and stake discovery claims with whatever other prospectors we pick up on the way in. That way we can get a mining district organized right away. I'd like to take Thunder and Lightning along. They'd be good in the bush, an' I could use 'em as messengers to come down to meet you."

"They're yours," Hedley said. "They've been all over that country, too. They'll scare hell outa any of them Stick injuns or Nenanas that might get in your way. The Chilkats got the 'skeer' on all them tribes." Then he changed the subject. "I aim to have enough stuff on them two boats o' mine to git our own town goin' and last one winter. With any luck, we might even make a second run before freeze-up. By the way, Dolf, I'd be glad to take Maggie and little Henry with me. It'd probably be easier on 'em. Skookum Doc here'd probably come along to look after 'em personally."

"Suits me," Doc agreed.

"It won't suit Maggie," Dolf said. "I already suggested it."

"How about yore hoss then?" Hedley asked. "Either that or we can leave 'im here. The mosquitoes 'n' black flies'll keep him miserable up there till freeze-up. Down here the wind blows 'em away most days. Besides, I don't think you'll have much use fer a hoss in there. We'll just hafta take up room carryin' feed up for 'im."

"I'm concerned about getting him regular exercise," Dolf said. "But you got a point about the feed business. Trouble is he won't let anybody except me and Jack's kid on him."

Old John stared up at the ceiling and blew a vast cloud of cigar smoke upward. "I hate to squeal on yore hoss, Dolf, but I do believe I've seen Elsie a-ridin' him around the corral a time or two. You know she's a Sioux. They can ride anything with ha'r on it."

"That rascal!" Dolf exclaimed. " 'An I thought he was a one-man animal. I guess that settles the hoss question. It's probably best all around to leave him here this season at least."

That was the last matter of business for that meeting. There would be others before their summer plans were all ironed out.

"By the way, Doc," Dolf said as they were breaking up. "How come yur trustin' a young sawbones to handle yore business, especially all that baby trade around Pinebluff. You may not be able to go back and face all them mamas you been handlin' for years."

Doc snorted. "Easy. He's pert near as good-lookin' as me. That goes a long ways with the gals. Besides, he went to the same medical school I did. Bound to be a genius."

"Medical school. Hell, I thought you picked it up in saloons an' like that," Dolf needled with a straight face.

"Only the gunshot and d.t. end of it," Doc said, unruffled. "Nobody better'n me at treatin' a case of the snakes or lead poisonin'. O' course, I got a lot of practice jist on you Morgettes alone."

Dolf took the good-natured insult silently. He'd seldom been more at ease.

This happy mood was shattered when, on the eve of their departure for Lake Bennett, Hedley called Dolf, Doc, and Quillen over for a meeting. He looked solemn.

"Bad news in the mail. Just to make sure that there wasn't even an outside chance the location of the Sky Pilot got away—since it ain't impossible something could happen to both me and Jack—I sent Ira Baker a map. He shoulda got it at least a month ago, but it never got there." He looked around gravely.

"How'd you send it?" Jack asked.

"Mailed it. A damn fool stunt on my part, I admit. But sendin' a messenger could have been just as risky. Besides, I couldn't spare anyone I'd trust."

"Damn," Jack said. "Of course mail gets lost lots of ways. Maybe it's just late."

"I'm hopin' it's late or lost, but we can't count on it. There's only one good thing about it. The map didn't have the actual location of the diggins on it. I sent Ira a special letter before then tellin' him the direction and distance of the actual location from where I was gonna put the X on the map I'd send later. He got that first letter okay."

"That's some consolation anyhow," Jack sighed.

"Some," John agreed. "But if Dwan thinks he don't need to depend on any of you fellers to lead him to the Sky Pilot, you'll *all* have to watch out for him every second. There's no tellin' where he'll try to hit you. And in any case, it'll be a race down the river now. If they got that map, and we have to figure they did to be on the safe side, you'll have to be even more on your guard. Soon enough we'll know. They'll try to hit us somewhere if they got it." He looked over at Dolf. "I reckon that'll change yore plans about takin' Maggie and the kid with you."

Dolf stared down at the table for a minute, then let out a short laugh. "It'll change my plans all right, but I'm bettin' it won't change hers—not unless I want to be single in a hurry." He paused. "She's as good as a man in a pinch. Proved it in Juneau. That wasn't any accident when she showed up coverin' our backs. As for the kid, he'll have something to tell his grandkids someday—we're gonna take the risks, whatever they are."

Old John nodded assent. He admired both Dolf and Maggie more than he'd ever admit. He'd have made the same decision himself if he and Elsie were concerned.

Dolf looked over at Doc. "What do you say, Skookum Doc?"

"Well," Doc said. "I learned to swim when I almost drowned runnin' you down the Mustang in that scow last spring. I say let's go!"

CHAPTER 9

GOLDIE sat at his big carved mahogany desk in the Skookum's second-floor office, his small, immaculately booted feet propped up on a partially opened drawer. He sucked on a long Perfecto and regarded Rudy Dwan speculatively with a languid, droop-lidded cast to his liquid black eyes.

Dwan had recognized a big change in Goldie since he'd returned from his enforced absence. He exuded brash confidence. The small, dapper conman lipped his cigar delicately now, getting ready to say something he obviously considered momentous. Dwan didn't care for Goldie; he especially disliked something about the clipped black beard and mustache that lent an ugly greedy appearance to the fat pink lips now enfolding the large cigar. But Dwan had learned discretion in years of working for men of Goldie's type. It didn't pay to reveal one's displeasure for even an instant, so he tried to appear respectively attentive.

Dwan figured Goldie's confidence probably stemmed from his having received full authority to manage the northern enterprise. He'd been gone long enough to visit Brown and Shadley in St. Louis; probably had, Dwan guessed. He thought, I wonder how they stomached the little bastard?

Goldie's first words interrupted this thought. "We've got the other side by the short hair." He paused for effect.

Dwan raised his eyebrows but maintained his silence, waiting for the big revelation that was undoubtedly about to come out.

"I know where the damn Lost Sky Pilot is located." He made it sound as though he'd discovered this information single-handedly.

Those St. Louis dudes have probably bribed someone to steal Ira Baker's mail again, Dwan surmised correctly.

"You know what that means? We can stop pussyfootin'

around. If anyone gets in our way, we can put 'em out of our way damn quick and not risk a thing."

He puffed rapidly on his cigar, looking slightly cross-eyed down its length to observe the fire going at its tip. He reminded Dwan of a pawnshop owner looking Christ-like while tapping his fingertips together and benignly offering ten-percent value for a stolen gold brick or some unfortunate's shirt. Dwan still did not offer comment.

Goldie continued, "We'll be in a race as soon as the ice goes out over on the Yukon. I want you and the boys to get over there in a few days to start building boats. I'll be over myself closer to breakup time."

That figures, Dwan thought. The little such-and-so will be goin' down to the Sky Pilot with us; he isn't about to tell anyone else where them diggins are located. Can't say as I blame him.

He knew *he* sure wouldn't if their positions were reversed. Yet he couldn't like anything about Goldie or his type. They were self-destructive—clever enough to see and grasp at the main chance, but so avaricious that it ultimately eluded them even when they perceived that they were condemning themselves to defeat. He wondered if Goldie recognized this trait in himself. "Half-smart" was the way Dwan rated him.

"That ain't all," Goldie went on, interrupting Dwan's train of thought. "I want you to bust up the other outfit's boats as fast as they build 'em. If someone gets hurt, too bad."

"That's easier said than done," Dwan spoke for the first time. "Morgette'll be over there for sure."

Goldie laughed. "We got an ace in the hole. Hedley hired some hands to help build them boats. Two of 'em are my boys. I suspect there's gonna be all sorts of bad luck over there. All you gotta do is a little drygulchin' if you get the chance. If we can pick off Morgette, our job'll be a hell of a lot simpler handlin' the rest of 'em. At any rate, even if they get the boats finished, they'll never make seven hundred miles down the river alive through all them injuns. Not after Hoonah Charlie gets 'em stirred up. As it was, we had to be sure at least Quillen got through. Now we don't need any of 'em. I want you to send old Hoonah Charlie's brother over there to get the new word to him. That whole bunch is fair game now!"

"How about Hedley and his two boats comin' up from St. Michael?" Dwan asked. "He just might beat us in there if the ice sticks in the upper Yukon a little late."

"I have a notion Old John's gonna have a lot of trouble with his project. We've had some old hands up at St. Michael all winter with our own boat-building crew. When them boats of Hedley's are just about ready to load, I suspect they might catch fire, or maybe blow up or something." He grinned wickedly, relishing the thought. "Couldn't happen to a nicer old s.o.b. than Old John. If something permanent happens to him in the bargain—and I told the boys it should—so much the better. I owe him plenty for shanghaing me outa here, although it turned out to be a good turn in the end. I got to see our big bosses. Got a free hand at this end. The gold don't interest 'em much. They want to control the trade on the whole Yukon. So they'll be buckin' the A.C. Co. as well as Baker 'n' Hedley. It oughta be some scrap. And we don't need to worry how the hell it comes out if our own little plan works. We win regardless of who else does." He chortled elatedly at the thought.

Dwan nodded agreement. "But," he said, "gettin' that gold out once we hijack it might not be so damn simple."

Goldie thought about that awhile, then said, "We don't hafta be in any hurry. We could even cache the stuff fer a coupla years an' lay low till the heat's off, long as no one finds out who's pullin' the heists."

Old John's Yukon expedition set out in early May from his trading post, bound for Lake Bennett. They were well prepared for the tortuous trail. Quillen and his son—as well as all the Chilkats—had been over the route many times before. The party included the Morgettes, Mama Borealis, Doc, four experienced boat builders, the Quillens, Thunder and Lightning, and a couple dozen Chilkat packers. The latter, like Old John's two, were all broad-shouldered, thickset with short sturdy legs, and able to bear a two-hundred-pound pack uphill and down all day long with scant rest. The party packed out through the canyon of the Dyea river, two miles long and perhaps fifty feet wide, strewn with boulders and deadfalls.

"Gotta be careful pretty soon," Quillen cautioned. "Plenty of avalanches in spring when we get heavy wet snows. A little late for that, thank God."

The pass above was fog-shrouded most of the time in winter. This day was bright and cloudless. Massive glaciers, frosty white with blue-green fissures, frowned broodingly above them. They had a grueling four miles facing them the next morning to reach the summit—which they managed by noon, due to an early start.

Dolf had insisted that Margaret walk each day after she was able, further each time, to harden her for this initial challenge. He was surprised to see how well she was doing, even when it was her turn to pack Henry. He had offered to do it as well as Margaret and Mama, or to have one of the Chilkats take Henry all the way, and had netted a withering look from his small wife.

When they finally topped out at the summit, they could see Dyea some thirty-five hundred feet below. Visible ahead was Lake Lindemann, twelve hundred feet lower down along their path. They pressed on to Lindemann and camped for the night. One relay of their packers had reached this point without stopping the previous day. They met them headed back for another load. Quillen had retained a half dozen with his immediate group to pack their camp equipment, and although he didn't mention it, to pack Margaret, too, if need be.

She'd probably drop from exhaustion first, thought Jack. It was a prospect he didn't relish. He was glad to see how well she stood up even under the last thirty-five-degree ascent to the summit. She'd got her breath at the top in short order, stopping to enjoy the view.

"What's that booming noise?" she asked Jack.

He pointed overhead. "The glacier. It shifts around. Sometimes it sounds like cannon when whatever's shifting is close. Every once in a while, something in there gives and a whole lake of water cuts loose and comes down. Time to head for the high ground when it does."

The next day they trudged down the shore of Lindemann on slushy ice most of the way, then made the last lap through the canyon to the head of Lake Bennett. There they planned to set up their boat-building operation. And there Dolf and Jack were certain they would sooner or later encounter Dwan—not openly of course, but from ambush. They were, as yet, unaware that his two saboteurs had been planted in their midst.

Their first task was establishing a weatherproof camp. Quillen had the boat builders set up pole frames for their tents, since a late blizzard might hit them with heavy arctic winds. Next he put them to work building sawpits, where they would whipsaw out ribs and planks for the boats. The lumber would be green and the boats sometimes leaky as a result. For that reason they carried plenty of extra caulking. Ample pitch was available from the pine trees growing in the vicinity. The boats themselves would be constructed from spruce.

The "sawpits" were raised scaffoldings on which a peeled log could be laid. Two men, one above and one below, would guide a six-foot, spike-toothed saw down a line chalked on the log. It was demanding work, fit to make a demon of an angel after a few hours. Cutting only occurred on the downward stroke, the man below doing the heavy work; the man above merely pulled the saw back up for another stroke. These experienced builders had brought goggles to keep the constant stream of sawdust out of the eyes of the man below. Two sawpits were erected, and everyone took turns on the top, where experience was not so essential. The lower man was the one who guided the saw along the chalk line. Notwithstanding the questionable dependability of two of the boat builders, they all obviously knew their business. This work went fast.

Meanwhile Dolf was having a systematic reconnaissance made of the surrounding area. He was certain that Brown and Shadley had, or soon would have, crews in the vicinity also engaged in boat building. If that were all he expected of them, he wouldn't have cared where they were, but he suspected Dwan would be with them. Although he'd stay under cover himself, Dwan's presence meant trouble. What he might be up to Dolf didn't know, but he prepared for the worst. If he'd known for sure that Goldie thought he had discovered the secret of the Sky Pilot's location, he'd have been no more careful than he was.

Dolf counted on Thunder and Lightning as his ace scouts. He wasn't disappointed. On their third day in camp, the two Chilkats reported back to him excitedly. Thunder, who was always the leader, said: "Dis inchen find um dem fella. Dey come watchum." He pointed to the crest above them. "Find dem track. Foller 'em." He pointed the way they went. "Up dat way."

Dolf called a powwow with Quillen, Doc, Ave, and the two Chilkats. To Jack he said, "I want you and Doc to stay here in case of unwelcome visitors. I'll take Ave for a little extra fire power if I need any and go scout out their operation. I particularly want to know if Dwan's over there."

Dolf wasn't sure what he would do if he discovered Dwan. His first inclination would probably be to walk straight in on him and gun him down. But Dolf was a careful man. He thought, Why tip my hand? Rudy can't be sure I'm after him personally. And I'm not dead mortal certain he plugged Harvey either. I'll be able to read it on his face when I finally brace him. Best give him a little rope and see what he tries.

The other camp was about halfway down the lake. Dolf studied it from cover on the timbered hill high above through a powerful pair of field glasses Old John had given him. There were at least a dozen people down there, and four tents were pitched. They also had double sawpits in operation. He searched in vain for a glimpse of Dwan, but saw no one resembling him. Finally he returned to his own camp, very slightly rewarded for a hard twenty-mile scout.

Quillen and Doc met him, eager for his report. He told them what he'd seen. "We don't even know they're our party," he said. "But I'd bet a new hat on it anyway. We'll keep a guard up on the hill. No tellin' what they might try to pull. If they got that map and actually think they don't need us to lead 'em in, they're apt to shoot up the place."

"I wish we knew for sure about that map," Jack said.

"Easy as hell to find out," Doc put in. He let that sink in.

"How?" Quillen asked.

"Sit here and see if they start out ahead of us. Let 'em stay ahead of us as far as that goes. Have less trouble with 'em that way."

Dolf didn't reply right away, making a final calculation of the advantages and drawbacks. "It'd be a big relief to know their game. If they got the map, I gotta watch out even sharper to keep all of us covered all the time. O' course, I'm doin' that anyway just in case, but it'd be nice to know for sure. I say let's let 'em pull out ahead of us if they want to. We'll just have to keep our eyes wide open. We'd have to do that for injuns anyhow. Besides, by then there should be some more parties comin' through after Old John spreads the word. We can count on some o' them against the injuns. Dwan's outfit—if it is Dwan's outfit—are gonna hesitate about killing if they think there's a lot of other witnesses that might stumble onto 'em in the act. I think, all in all, we oughta let them make the first move."

Their first move came quicker than he expected. The next morning Dolf, Doc, and Jack were having a morning smoke after breakfast when a bullet whizzed past them. The long delay before they heard the report told them the gunman was far off. They'd been seated beside the lake on a low rock ledge, beneath which they now quickly took cover. A second and third shot followed. Then they heard a new gun join in from another location. This time no bullets came their way.

"Ave," Quillen said, referring to his boy on guard up above. "Good boy."

Obviously, whoever had slipped up hadn't known Ave was there, but neither had Ave been able to spot him first. The nature of the terrain made that extremely difficult.

Under cover of Ave's shooting, Doc and Jack ran to get their rifles. Dolf had had his rifle leaning on the ledge beside him. He peeked over the ledge and scanned the hillside carefully. A running figure was scampering for the crest, and Ave's rifle blasted again, but whoever it was kept going. Dolf pumped two long-range shots from his .45-90 at the runner before he got over the ridge. The range was at least six hundred yards —too long for real accuracy, especially on a running shot.

When Doc and Jack got back, Dolf was standing up, reloading.

"Gone," Dolf said. "I'm goin' after him. I want Thunder along to track. And Doc, you come along to pay a little visit with me in case he leads us where I think he will."

Doc said, "I'm your man. I'll get my scattergun if it's gonna be the kind of party I think it is."

"How about us?" Quillen asked, referring to himself and his son, but also to the boat-building crew, who were coming over to see what the shooting was all about.

"I want the camp covered. That shooting may have been to decoy us away so someone could slip in and maybe burn us out."

The gunman had done his best to stick to rocky ground and spots where there was little snow left. However, it hadn't been entirely possible. Perhaps recognizing that, he had finally taken to a small glacial stream that had already thawed. There the trail ended. Dolf looked up the hill, then down. "I'm bettin' he ain't up there. Let's try the other way."

No tracks emerged from the stream at any point all the way down to the lake. The rivulet flooded out onto the lake ice, covering it for several hundred yards with a few inches of water.

"Just on a hunch, let's head toward that other camp and see if our friend's tracks show up somewhere," Dolf said.

They were rewarded at last with a set of tracks along the shore. In the slush, they couldn't be sure they were the same tracks, however. Even Thunder wasn't certain. "I tink mebbe so," he said. "Mebbe no. No good."

"What do you think, Doc?"

"Can't say. Let's circle around and pay those guys a visit anyhow. They'll be watchin' for us to come this way if they're watchin'."

Doc proved to be a prophet. They were able to walk right into the other camp after making a long two-hour detour to approach it from down the lake. A substantial clump of spruce surrounding the camp helped to conceal them. The first man to spot them was just coming from under the flap of one of the tents. Dolf brought his rifle to bear on him. It was Dwan.

"Rudy!" Dolf said.

Dwan looked up startled, the look changing to fear almost at once. He turned pale.

"No, Dolf," he said, "I didn't. . . ." Then he stopped to think what he was saying and how Dolf would take it; he let the sentence trail off. By then some of Dwan's men woke up to what was going on.

"What the hell!" one of them exclaimed.

"Don't anybody reach for anything," Doc warned sweeping the double barrel over everyone in sight.

"Call off your boys, Rudy," Dolf ordered. "You'll be the first one dead if anybody starts anything."

Dwan was relieved that Dolf hadn't necessarily come to kill him.

"It's okay!" Dwan yelled. "They wanna talk."

"I oughta shoot you in your tracks, Rudy. What were you gonna say—you didn't what?"

"You know what. Why should I lie? I didn't kill Harvey

Parrent. But I knew everybody'd think I did. I knew you'd be after me, so I pulled out."

Dolf tried to read his face. He was either mighty smooth, or telling the truth. "Who did kill Harvey?"

"I don't know, Dolf. And that's the God's truth."

Dolf half-believed him. In any case this wasn't the place to settle that score. He wanted to get Dwan alone someday.

"We'll see about that some other time," Dolf said. "That ain't what I came about. Somebody took a coupla shots into my camp a while back. I came here to tell you I can't prove someone from here did it, but if it happens again, I'll be over and shoot up this place every day on general principles. My wife and baby are over there, and another woman."

"I knew you were over there," Dwan admitted. "But I sure didn't know there was women and a baby with yuh."

"Does that mean you did that shootin'?"

"Hell no," Dwan said, frightened all over again. "Coulda been injuns. They're on the prod all over here. Too many whites comin' in to suit them."

"Wasn't an injun's track, and we followed it this way. You've had fair warning, Rudy. If I hafta come back, it won't be talkin'."

"All right, Dolf. It wasn't anybody from here, though. And I can promise it won't be. Especially not with women and a baby over there."

Dolf and Doc backed away, joining Thunder in the spruce thicket where he'd covered their backs. They went back the way they'd come.

"So that's Dwan," Doc said. "Why didn't yuh burn him down?"

"The sign wasn't right. I want to get him alone. Besides, I halfway believe him. Either he's tellin the truth—he didn't back-shoot Harvey—or he's the smoothest liar I ever saw."

CHAPTER 10

GOLDIE Smith showed up a lot earlier than Dwan had expected.

"Hedley run in a cold deck on us," Goldie explained, sounding bitter. "He told the whole world that Quillen discovered the Lost Sky Pilot and is headed in to locate on it. They'll be two hundred prospectors here inside a week if I'm any judge."

That explained why Goldie had brought in two dog teams. He set the boat builders to work at once on sleds, supervised by two Canuck dog-team drivers he'd brought in with him.

"Maybe I can get a head start with dogs. I'll take them two Canucks and two of the boat builders and git as far down as I can on the ice. It ain't rubbery yet. Where it is, it still freezes solid at night. If we can get below White Horse Rapids before we run outa good travelin' ice, we can throw together a boat down there and beat everyone in."

"What are yuh plannin' to do about Quillen and Morgette now?" Dwan wanted to know. He told Goldie about the complication of two women and a baby being over there.

The little schemer turned that over in his mind rapidly. "I'd still like to put Morgette and Quillen outa the way permanent, but we got a new deal. For the time being, leave 'em to my boys that are supposedly buildin' their boats. At the right time they'll keep 'em outa the race. If we was to get involved in shootin' and them women or the kid got hurt, now that a bunch of miners are comin' in we might just stretch rope. We'll let the injuns settle their hash later; maybe do it ourselves an' make it look like an injun job."

"You ain't plannin' to let the injuns beef them two gals and a baby, are yuh?" Dwan complained.

There was a wicked speculative gleam in Goldie's eyes for just a moment, then, sensing Dwan's disapproval, he quickly turned on a disarming smile. But he also made a note that

Rudy would bear watching. He was a good man to have, but not necessarily indispensable, although few other musclemen he could get would have Rudy's brains.

"Well?" Dwan pressed for an answer.

"Shucks, no," Goldie said smoothly. "I was just blowin' off a little steam. It won't hurt to let 'em get to the diggins anyhow, after we got it all filed on." But he was thinking, If the injuns fall down on the job and we hafta take care of Morgette and Co. ourselves, I'll have to make sure Rudy's somewhere else. I sure don't want Morgette running the law end of any town where I aim to set up business.

"You been in touch with our boys over in Quillen's camp?" Goldie asked.

"You bet. One of 'em goes out hunting every once in a while when he gets a few hours. He even got a moose his first time out so nobody's suspicious of him. I meet him a couple of times a week."

"What they plannin' on doin' to stop Morgette and that crew?"

"They've been watchin' fer a chance to accidentally-on-purpose drop a log or somethin' on Dolf. They aim to burn the boats, or set 'em adrift after they're finished, so they'll have to build another pair. That could set 'em back a couple of weeks, I guess."

"Good," Goldie said. "That's the ticket. Even if they all git through, God forbid, the main thing is to beat 'em to the diggins. Brown and Shadley may figure the way to get richer is trading, but I got my eye on the gold."

That made sense to Dwan. He was relieved that Goldie didn't insist on any more bushwhacking attempts. Dwan couldn't exactly be accused of hiding a heart of gold behind his rough ways, but he had a soft spot for kids and the frontiersman's respect for "good" women.

Dolf had learned from bitter past experience to keep an eye

on everyone and to trust very few. He had his suspicions who had fired those three shots into their camp—Dwan himself, he'd bet. In fact, he'd had a notion to look into that tent Dwan had come out of to see if he could find a pair of soaked mukluks. Despite Dwan's assurances—given under duress, a fact also to be considered—Dolf thereafter placed Thunder or Lightning on the ridge above camp at all times. He and the two Quillens and Doc alternated at regular spells of patrol duty there, too, so there were always two people on guard. It had also occurred to him from the very first that he really knew nothing of the four boat builders. He intended to keep only the two who were experienced white-water men and send the other two back to Juneau as soon as they were no longer needed. It made two less to keep an eye on. They were all good, willing workers, and he'd seen nothing to arouse his suspicions about any of them. Jack had, of course, discharged the Chilkat packers as soon as the last load of supplies was in, so at least there were none of them to worry over.

Greg Jackson had turned out to be a lucky hunter as well as a good boat builder. The big bull moose he'd brought down had kept them in meat for several days. Quillen, as a result, allowed Jackson to go hunting whenever he could be spared. It had taken only a week to rough-cut enough planks and ribbing, so with the four-man job over Jackson could be more readily spared to hunt. The days were growing long and, with little else to do, the builders were more than willing to work twelve hours daily with only time out for meals, since they were on hourly wages. The next stage of the building would be planing down the lumber.

Everyone was enjoying the camp. The lake, about a mile wide here at its southern end, was surrounded by steep, wooded hills. At some places cliffs dropped to the water's edge. Here and there rivulets of melted snow were starting down the hills, making an occasional waterfall. Dolf found little time for enjoying it, however. His time was divided between turns on guard duty, shifts with the boat builders, and trying to get enough sleep during the day to stand night guard during the few hours of darkness.

One of Dolf's problems solved itself by sheer luck. Ave, who was up on the ridge on patrol one day, knew that Jackson wanted to bag a caribou. Ave had brought down many of the big animals, having got his first when he was only twelve. So when he spotted one crossing the ridge above camp, he thought of Jackson, whom he'd seen leave earlier to hunt somewhere over on the other side. He figured he could circle with the wind on the caribou, then try to find Jackson and guide him to where he could get a shot. Bush-wise Ave stumbled across Jackson meeting Rudy Dwan, but had been moving so cautiously from habit that neither of them saw him. He slipped as close to them as he could, undetected. At first he'd assumed Jackson had probably run across some one of their own party, but he soon learned better. He'd seen the photos of Rudy Dwan and surmised what was going on. Unfortunately, the open terrain prevented him from getting close enough to hear what was said.

He thought, I kin figure what they're sayin'. We got a skunk in camp fer sure.

He continued to watch till he was absolutely certain the two weren't planning to slip over and shoot them up again. He was wise enough not to jump them, though he wasn't afraid of trying it. Might not learn nearly as much that way, he reasoned. Best I just let Dolf and Paw figure out how to handle it.

After Dwan and Jackson separated, Ave remained under cover until they were well out of sight. Then he followed Jackson, soon overtaking him.

"Hey, Mr. Jackson," he yelled. Jackson looked startled as he turned and recognized Ave, then tried to assume a nonchalant appearance.

"Hi, Ave," he said. "What're you doin'?"

"I seen a big caribou come over the ridge. Figgered you

might get that shot at one yuh bin wantin'. He's over that-away." He pointed down the ridge. "Yuh got the wind on 'im from here. Oughta be able to slip up on 'im if yuh go slow."

He watched Jackson disappear, slipping among the spruce and aspen down the ridge, then quickly made his way toward camp. He told Dolf what he'd discovered. After a while Dolf called both Quillen and Doc over for a confab. He had waited awhile because he knew Greg Jackson and Sam Murphy, one of the other builders, were pretty thick. Just in case they were in cahoots, he didn't want Sam making any shrewd surmises about a confab being called right after Ave busted out of the brush looking like he had some big news. If both Jackson and Murphy were tools of Dwan's, it was a cinch Murphy'd know why Greg was out in the bush. Dolf wanted to have a little talk with Greg before he ran him off.

When Doc and Jack joined him, Dolf told them, "Ave just came down and told me something powerful interesting. He spotted Greg Jackson and Rudy Dwan havin' a little confab up yonder." He motioned up the ridge. "Mebbe they're old friends and just happened to run into each other."

"Yah," Quillen put in, "and maybe robins weigh forty pounds."

"More likely, though," Dolf went on, "Dwan or Goldie planted him on us. He's pretty damn close to Murphy, too. Maybe we got two Judases in our camp. Whatever the case is, I'm gonna have a little come-to-Jesus meeting with Greg Jackson and then send 'im back to Juneau. Might do the same for Murphy, depending on whether he looks guilty when we brace his sidekick."

"I'd hate ta lose 'em both," Jack said. "They're the two that know how to run white water. Without 'em we'll be in a real pickle gettin' through Miles and Whitehorse."

Dolf had considered that. "We'd probably never get there, much less through, with them around—not that I'm con-demning Murphy without a fair hearing. But if they're workin' fer Dwan, we can figure they'll try something underhanded every step of the way to take us outa the race. They don't know the real show don't start without us gettin' there."

"Why don't we just put a rope around both their necks and see how long they can stand on their toes," Doc suggested. "Funny how a fella gets a powerful urge ta sing under them particular circumstances, as I recall."

"In any case," Dolf said, ignoring Doc's suggestion, "I ain't plannin' to run Jackson off till mornin'. I want him far away as possible by tomorrow night. We'll herd him to the top of Chilkoot and prod him over."

"I think we oughta herd 'em both over," Doc said. "Birds of a feather."

"I'd hate to do that unless we're powerful sure," Quillen objected. "You ain't never seen them rapids we gotta take our boats through. We'll really need someone that knows their onions—or a powerful damn lot of luck. Wouldn't do to get stranded down there with our supplies on the bottom of the river. We'd starve before we got out if the huntin' turned sour. I've gone a couple of weeks in that country without seein' even a rabbit. Other times yuh have to kick your way through the game. There ain't no predictin' it."

"Well," Dolf said. "Let's just see how Murphy acts when we run off his pal."

Jackson came in without having bagged his caribou. Dolf wondered if maybe he had something else on his mind. He was especially alert that night, thinking it would be a helluva shame if they got burned out just about the time they were ready to eliminate a possible saboteur. He waited till after breakfast before calling all the men in the party together—except Lightning, who was on guard.

Without preamble he said, "I thought you all might like to hear what Greg here has to say about what he was talkin' about to Rudy Dwan over the other side of the ridge yesterday."

Jackson looked like a man who'd just taken a solar plexus punch. He was speechless.

"You got anything to say, Greg?" Dolf asked with deceptive mildness.

Greg Jackson was obviously racking his brain furiously to find a way out. Finally, unable to alibi himself, he shrugged his shoulders and grinned. "What the hell," he said. "I been caught. I needed the money. I got a wife and two babies back in Seattle. They gotta eat. It looked like a lot of money to me. I never had a hundred dollars all at once in my whole life. I never got a cent of it myself. Sent it all home." He looked embarrassed.

"What'd they pay you the hundred to do?" Dolf asked.

"Well, when the boats were finished we . . . I mean I was supposed to burn 'em, or cut 'em loose, or sink 'em. Anything to hold you fellers up from gettin' started down the river."

Dolf looked over at Murphy. "You heard that 'we' business. He wouldn't happen to have meant you, would he? You two seem to be mighty thick."

Murphy looked blank. "This whole thing is news to me."

Dolf shot at Jackson, "How about it? You gonna take the rap all by yourself? Get the rope, Doc. I'm gonna take your suggestion. This is one bastard that ain't gonna cause us any more trouble."

"What the hell ya plannin' ta do?" Jackson yelled. "I admit I took some money from Goldie Smith. But Mary and the babies'll starve if you swing me. Goddam, I ain't killed anybody or anything!"

Dolf was poker-faced. "Get the rope, Doc."

Jackson's eyes blazed. "You guys can go to hell. I ain't done nothin' anybody else wouldn't have done if they was up against it."

Dolf looked over at Murphy. "You can save your pal by speakin' up about now."

Murphy exploded. "You're all crazy."

"Let's swing him, too," Doc suggested.

"I read about you two in the papers," Murphy said. "I didn't believe it. You both must be nuts."

The other two boat builders stood by, open-mouthed. Finally Windy Montgomery said, "Are you serious about this, Morgette?"

Dolf grinned a little. "Hell no. I just wanted to see if both these boys were in this together. It looks like they weren't, I guess, or one of 'em woulda sung before now." Then, turning to Greg, he said, "Get your outfit together. I want you on the other side o' Chilkoot by dark."

He drew Greg to one side for a moment. He fished in his pocket and drew out a roll of crumpled bills, offering it to Jackson. "For Mary and them babies," he said.

Jackson flushed deeply, looking down at his boots. Then he looked Dolf straight in the eye. "Hell, Morgette," he said, smiling. "I ain't never been married in my life."

Dolf laughed suddenly. He clapped Jackson on the shoulder. "You're a damn fine liar then. One o' the best I've seen."

Jackson offered his hand. "You're a good man, Morgette. Good luck."

CHAPTER 11

THE boats were both finished and looked as fine and sturdy as any Dolf had seen along the waterfront in Portland. They'd been designed in Eb Frazer's head. Eb had been Quillen's straw boss on the job. Since Jackson's banishment, the builders remaining were Eb, Murphy, and Windy Montgomery (who'd got his nickname from his claim that George Washington was his grandfather and, moreover, had won the battle of Bunker Hill — at which almost everyone else knew Washington hadn't been present). At any rate, Windy was good at his trade and proud of the two boats. They had four feet of freeboard at the bow, three amidships, and gracefully curved up to about three and a half at the stern, which tapered to a point. Their bottoms were flat, and they ran about five feet in the beam at the widest point of their twenty-foot length. Everyone was standing around admiring the finished products, which were laid upside down on sawhorses after their final caulking.

"Them babies'll carry eight tons apiece before you'd sink 'em to the gunn'les," Eb stated proudly. "They can carry our outfits and the bunch of us and still float like corks."

Quillen was a little embarrassed to have to throw cold water on Eb's enthusiasm, since he'd come to like him real well. "Uh, Eb," he started, "we wasn't figurin' on you and Windy comin' along. I'da mentioned it sooner if I thought you didn't know."

Eb looked crestfallen. Embarrassed, he looked down at his boots, but all he managed to say was, "Oh."

Windy wasn't to be put off that easily. "Hell, Jack, we'd just have to go back to Dyea or Juneau and outfit to come back over. We don't aim to miss this big strike. How about we pay you to take us in with yuh, or somethin'? We done a good job fer yuh — we don't deserve to git shoved out now so's we'd be at the tail end of the crowd that's on their way over. Hell fire, we got a half dozen camps up and down here already a-buildin' boats like crazy. Besides, yuh might need a few extra rifles if we run across them injuns old Hoonah Charlie's supposed to be a-steamin' up."

Eb looked hopefully at Quillen. Jack looked at Dolf for some sign of how he might be disposed toward the proposition. Seeing he was expected to make the decision, Dolf said, "It makes good sense to me, Jack. Besides, these boys have done a damn good job for us. It's okay with me if it is with you."

"It's a deal," Jack agreed. "Only yuh don't have to pay us anything. You'll earn your keep if I'm any judge. We may need them Winchesters."

That night Dolf settled down to his first good sound sleep since they'd been there. Margaret had made them a comfortable mattress of Spruce branches, carefully sorting out only the soft spongy tips. There wasn't a lump in the whole affair. Their bedding consisted of two eiderdown pillows and a blanket-lined wolfskin sleeping bag that Elsie Hedley had spent a month sewing together for them. There was nothing warmer or more frost-resistant. Henry D. was snug next to them in his cradle. They shared their tent with Mama Borealis, whom they knew wouldn't be happy more than a few feet from the baby at night.

Dolf instantly recognized that something was wrong as soon as he woke up. They usually left their campfire to burn down by itself, but the reflected flames were too bright for that.

The boats! Dolf thought. Someone set 'em on fire.

He grabbed a six-shooter in case that someone was still around, then rushed outside barefoot, in his longjohns.

"Stay there, Maggie," he ordered as she tried to go with him. "Don't come out just yet."

Eb Frazer was coming out of his tent at the same time. "Fire!" he yelled. Without waiting for anyone to respond, he grabbed a bucket and headed the few feet to the hole they'd chopped in the ice at the edge of the lake. Dolf grabbed another and joined him, but at the same time he was aware that they were sitting ducks in the firelight if the arsonists were hidden in the nearby woods.

"We'll just hafta risk it," he thought. "By now they'd have at least shot at me for sure."

In moments the whole camp was up. The fires were directly on top of the upturned boats and spreading rapidly. Someone had apparently set a bonfire on each of them. The thought passed through Dolf's mind that it had to have been someone Jim Too knew or he'd have given the alarm. The flames were stubborn, persisting even after the bonfires stoking them had been shoveled off the boat bottoms onto the ground.

"Coal oil," Quillen yelled. "Keep the water comin'."

A bucket brigade managed to get enough water on the twin fires to eventually extinguish the last ember.

Even as he'd been helping put out the fires, Dolf had also been taking a mental roll call of who was present or, more importantly, who wasn't. If the arsonist hadn't cut out, it would be hard to pin it on anyone, even though he was sure it had to be an inside job.

Murphy, he thought. Murphy ain't here.

He hadn't been the only one thinking that. When the last ember had died, Quillen ranged up beside him. "Murphy's gone," he said.

"So I noticed," Dolf responded. "Maybe headed after his pal. More likely went over to join Dwan's outfit."

Their shouts and the fire had attracted a crowd from the other nearby camps; at least a dozen men had shown up. "What happened, Jack?" one of them asked Quillen.

"Someone tried to burn us out."

Eb had produced a hurricane lamp. "It's a mess," he moaned. "Damn near burned through the bottom on both of 'em."

"Who the hell'd do a thing like that?" another of the newcomers asked.

Quillen briefly told the group of newcomers about Murphy

and his pal Jackson and that they worked for Goldie and Dwan.

"I know Murphy," someone said. "How kin you be sure it was him? Maybe he caught somebody in the act and is laid out cold somewhere around here?"

"Fat chance, Stan," retorted Quillen. "He'll either be headed for the outside or over to Dwan's camp. I say we oughta go over and pay those boys a visit. If we don't put a stop to this kind of thing now, none of us'll be safe."

The man Quillen called Stan was Stanley King, a well-known old-timer who was generally respected. The newcomers obviously looked to him for their lead in this business. There had been a ripple of voices agreeing with Quillen's suggestion till King said, "Hold on, Jack. I'd go easy with that kinda talk. There ain't no proof it was Murphy—or, for that matter, that he's in cahoots with anybody. I don't know Dwan, but if he works for Goldie, he'll have some tough boys with him. There could be shootin' if we horned in over there."

"Damn right," Quillen said. "And I'm all for it." He related how Goldie had tried to sweat the secret of Sky Pilot out of him.

"I heard about that, Jack. It was pretty raw. But I heard about you boys shanghaing Goldie, too. I don't aim to rake anybody's chestnuts till I know more about it."

Quillen bristled over that. "Well, if that's the way you feel, I sure as hell take the invitation back."

Windy broke into the conversation, announcing, "It was Murphy, all right. He's gone and most of his stuff is gone. He musta packed it on the sly, ready to scram. I'm bettin' he headed over to Dwan's."

Nobody seemed to be able to think of a reply to that. Finally Dolf said, "Let's forget it for now. We got work to do gettin' those boats repaired. We can handle Murphy's case some other time."

"You're Morgette, I guess," Stan said. "King's my name. Been up here ten years, just like Jack."

He offered his hand and Dolf shook it, thinking, That's a funny sort of way to introduce himself.

King soon made his purpose clear. "We do things a little different up in this country, as Jack probably told you."

"What the hell does that mean?" Quillen interrupted.

"Just friendly advice, Jack." He saw that he might have said too much to a man like Dolf. He quickly changed the subject. "If you gents need any help, just holler."

"I did holler," Quillen retorted acidly. "But I sure as hell didn't get any help. I'm thinkin' maybe I'll go back outside and take a vacation this season. I never wanted to get rich anyhow."

"Wait a minute!" someone yelled. "You ain't serious, are you?"

"Serious as hell," Quillen said. "Country's changin'. Gittin' too lawless fer an old cuss like me."

"Hey, Stan," this man said, "see what your damn wishy-washy bull can do for us? Anybody but a simpleton knows Goldie Smith is crooked as a sidewinder."

Stan King didn't reply, stalking away from the group in a huff.

"Cool down," Quillen said. "I was only needling the old bastard. And thanks for the support." In a louder voice he said, "Thanks for comin' over, boys. Ain't anything more to do right now. Anybody wants to stay for coffee is plumb welcome."

Mama Borealis and Margaret had set about heating the big coffeepot as soon as the boat fires had been put out. But no one took the invitation. The men drifted back to their camps, some yawning.

Doc hadn't said a word till then. He'd heard of miner's meetings all his life in the West and had his own opinion about how they'd work. He'd just had that opinion confirmed.

"If that's the backbone of law and order in this country," he snorted, "I'm sure glad I cut my teeth on a six-shooter. I never yet heard of a committee beatin' anyone to the draw."

"The boys'll come through in a real pinch," Quillen told him.

"Yah," Doc retorted. "An' if I'm any judge, a real pinch is when their own ox gets gored damn bad and not before."

Dolf merely shrugged. He'd seen and heard it all before. Somewhere deep inside, he sensed he was growing tired of it all. Most of the troubles in his life had come from single-handedly shouldering the law-and-order responsibility in communities too lily-livered to fight their own battles. Well, he thought. I'm in it again now. But this may be the last time. I've about got my belly full of it.

He'd seen plenty of other judicious-appearing asses like Stanley King who always sat around solemn as a goose trying to hatch a porcelain doorknob, piously convincing themselves that their indecisiveness was actually even-handedness, then learned their mistake too late. When they did, they usually came running to him. Dolf thought, He won't be any exception either, I'll bet. King would be all righteous indignation if an outrage was pulled off on him.

The main thing now was to repair the boats. This was neatly handled by Eb and Windy right on time for the ice breakup. They launched the boats as soon as there was clear water and tried the oars. The boats handled well and were thoroughly watertight. At Quillen's insistence, they'd also installed demountable masts.

"Get some extra speed on the lakes," Jack said. "Seen it done before up here."

It was the fifteenth of June when they set off down the lake. The last of the ice pack was running several days ahead of them, due to the delay. It had probably been out for several weeks further down. The day was ideal for setting sail. Lake Bennett was as smooth as glass, although frequent arctic tempests often rendered it hazardous to small craft. Jack Quillen, who had been over this route several times before by water, was in the lead boat. With him were his son, Doc, Lightning, and Windy Montgomery. Dolf, the women, his son, Thunder, and Eb were in the boat following. Instructed by Jack, they raised the sails, which augmented the current's speed considerably.

For the first fifteen miles or so, Jack kept them hugging the left shore, the wooded hills gliding past above them. On their way Dolf scanned the far shore with his field glasses for signs of Dwan's camp. It was gone, as he'd expected. They were probably days ahead.

"See anything?" Quillen yelled across.

"They're gone," Dolf yelled back.

"Good riddance," Quillen replied. "But you can bet we ain't seen the last of 'em."

About five miles further down, Jack steered straight across to the east shore. "Safest thing to do," he yelled back. "See that rough choppy water up there ahead? Always a big wind out of the west arm about here. Comes right down from the mountains."

As they crossed the arm, sticking to the lee shore, the austere, remote peaks of the coast range, shining like alabaster, were visible far up to the west, standing tall on the horizon, tops shrouded by pearly clouds. Glacial winds churned the lake's surface here, abating somewhat before they reached the east shore. They arrived at the foot of the lake in about five hours, beached for lunch, then pushed on an hour later through Three Mile River into Tagish Lake.

Jack had warned them of the hazards of Tagish Lake. "Windy Arm comes in from the south. Lots of greenhorns been swamped there and drowned. Best to stick to the north shore past there."

It turned out to be an ideal day for navigating the upper lake system. Tagish Lake, twenty miles long, required roughly another four hours to get through. Everyone was enjoying the scenery and weather. As the boats sailed almost abreast for a while, Jack yelled, "Usually a bunch of injuns through here. We ain't seen a one. I don't like that. Something may be in the wind. I hope not, but I got a funny feelin' in my bones."

Of course, the whole party knew that Hoonah Charlie had probably been through this country on his troublemaking errand, so Jack's message was perfectly clear. Leaving Tagish Lake, they made it down Four Mile River, after which Jack headed ashore to camp for the night on the west bank of Marsh Lake. The sandy bar he selected for their camping spot offered exposure to the wind, which would blow away the ever-present arctic mosquitoes. More importantly, though, it offered a clear view of the approaches to their camp from all directions.

Everyone had begun to feel a sense of foreboding that the Indian threat was bound to materialize soon. The brooding dark forests that encircled them seemed impenetrable and threatening.

Dolf had given a good deal of thought to their best course of action in case they did encounter the hostile natives. He had discussed the matter with everyone several times. "We don't want to start shooting unless we have to, but if it looks like they're gonna cut loose, get in the first shot. I don't aim to get any of us killed waitin' to find out their game. But let's not forget that Thunder and Lightning here may be able to argue some sense into 'em. That, and we've got enough supplies to give them lots of presents, especially grub. Never saw an injun yet that wasn't hungry." He looked at Margaret and grinned, then added slyly, "Especially if it's a pregnant mama."

"Uhn," Margaret agreed obligingly, if a trifle sarcastically.

Using the mosquito netting Quillen had brought along in large quantities, they were able to rig the boats for comfortable sleeping. These marquisette curtains had been developed by the British in India. They were a godsend to Margaret for protecting little Henry. She came from a mosquito country where there had been no means of protection except smudge fires or smothering under blankets at night, even if it was stifling hot.

The anticipated Indian threat did not materialize at this location. After breakfast, before shoving off again, Quillen privately aired his fears to Dolf. "I 'spect we'll see our injuns sure at the head of Miles Canyon. That's the one place they know we'll come ashore. Same goes for Dwan and his outfit if they're fixin' to drygulch us. I say Canyon Head is where we'll run into our first big trouble if we're gonna run into any. But I don't see any way o' dodgin' it. We gotta stick to the river. An' it's a cinch we better land there and scout the water from the bank. There's a dozen miles through there of the worst water on the river in Miles Canyon and White Horse Rapids. Lots of boys been drowned in there, or if they were lucky just lost their outfits. If the water looks too bad, we can pack around and let the boats run through empty. Trouble is that might hold us up a week at least. I sure as hell wish we hadn't lost them two white-water men." He shrugged. "So be it. We'll make the best of a bad deal."

Dolf agreed. His whole adult life had so far consisted of meeting a series of potentially hazardous or fatal threats. He shrugged his shoulders. "We'll either make it or we won't, Jack. Life's a gamble. We'll give it our best shot."

As they sailed down Marsh Lake, he pushed the future from his mind, enjoying the scenery and the company of his family. If Margaret was worried, she didn't show it any more than he did.

She's like me, he thought. Seen so much trouble she don't worry about it till it camps on the doorstep.

It took them most of the day to make it across Marsh Lake to where the river proper started, then on down to the head of Miles Canyon, where they landed on the left bank.

"We'll have plenty of light to scout the canyon on the bank," Jack said, "but I don't think we'd better try to get through before morning. Best we camp here."

It was then that his prophecy paid off. An Indian appeared on the bank above them, then another; in a few moments there were at least two dozen of them, all packing rifles. Dolf looked them over; they were standing silently, making no threatening motions as yet. He quickly scanned the far bank with the notion of retreating to that side. This possibility had obviously occurred to the Indians. There were almost an equal number of them lining that bank. Their only avenue of retreat, down through Miles Canyon, was one that was potentially more threatening than the Indians, who didn't seem inclined to start shooting just yet. Besides, the boats were pulled well up on the bank and moored to trees; it would take a couple of minutes to shove off.

"Let them make the first move," Dolf cautioned. "If there's going to be shooting, wait'll I start it. Everyone get into the boats and stay down; they're our best cover if we have to shoot it out. Keep your Winchesters handy."

A new figure joined the silent band of Indians on the hill above them. They made way for him as though they'd been expecting him.

"Dat Hoonah Charlie," Thunder told Dolf. "Big medicine. I shoot dat inchen, dem damn Stick inchen all run like hell."

Thunder raised the Winchester that Old John had loaned him for the trip. The Indians on the hill all started to scatter.

"Don't shoot, Thunder," Dolf ordered. He noted with satisfaction, however, that the Indians had started to scatter. Some, in fact, had run behind the hill.

"See," Thunder said. "Inchen scared like hell ub Chilkat. Kick ass plenty. Dem all same scared."

Hoonah Charlie waved his arms. "No shoot!" he yelled. "Make talk."

Dolf motioned him on down. Some of the other Indians gained confidence and followed him as he came closer.

"Watch for a trick, Dolf," Doc cautioned. "They may wanta get close enough to gang us."

"I don't think so," Dolf said. "There's something funny here I don't get."

As they came closer, Dolf said, "Charlie, you tell those others to stay back." He motioned with his arm to emphasize his demand.

Thunder also said something to them in their own language

and raised his Winchester threateningly again. Charlie's followers stopped, letting him come forward alone. Dolf noted that Charlie's face was grotesquely distended on one side. Something was obviously wrong with him.

Charlie pointed to his swollen face, addressing Dolf. "One big damn toot'ache. You got Skookum Doc, all same fixum squaw wit' bebby?"

So, Dolf thought, the shoe's on the other foot. This damn fraud knows I ain't bad medicine like he's been tellin' these fool injuns, or he wouldn't be down here askin' for help.

Doc motioned Charlie over to his boat. "I'm Skookum Doc," he said, pointing his thumb at his chest. "Come over here."

"Before you help the old scoundrel out," Dolf said, "we'll make him promise to tell his Indians I ain't bad medicine." Turning to Thunder, he told him to give Hoonah Charlie the message to make sure he got it through his head. After Thunder talked to Hoonah Charlie, the medicine man harangued his Indians for a while in their tongue.

"Make him send somebody to that bunch of his on the other side and get them the word too," said Dolf. Charlie readily agreed to that as well.

Doc got his dentistry tools out, which he kept like most frontier doctors who had to double as dentists (and sometimes vice versa) due to the shortage of either. He soon had Hoonah Charlie sitting in a folding camp chair and was ready to give him a big whiff of nitrous oxide. The curious band of Indians unconsciously shuffled closer to watch, fascinated by this strange ritual of Skookum Doc, whom they'd heard of by way of the mysterious wilderness grapevine.

"Wait'll he gets the giggles," Doc said. "I'll really be big medicine when they see somebody with a bad toothache laughing. They don't call it laughing gas for nothing."

He prodded around in Charlie's mouth till the gas-happy Indian confirmed which tooth it was.

"Big abscessed molar," Doc grunted. "Jeezuz, this bastard smells worse'n Limburger cheese."

Satisfied that Charlie was suitably anesthetized, Doc said to Jack, "You hold him in that chair tight." He drew a big pair of extracting forceps from his kit, propped Charlie's mouth wide open, and firmly attached them. Then he bore down with an expert, sharp twisting motion and pried upward. The tooth came out clean. Doc held it up in the forceps for all the Indians to see. Then he went to work cleaning up the infection with alcohol on cotton swabs. Charlie had shown no evidence of pain during the operation, a fact that caused a great deal of interest and excitement among the gathered tribesmen, who were poking each other, gesticulating and jabbering about it.

But the popular part of the treatment with the patient was the tin cup of whiskey Doc proffered him when it was all over. He downed it quickly. "Ahhh," he said, smacking his lips. By this time the Sticks had all crowded around Doc, eying his whiskey supply hopefully.

"Watch out, Doc," Jack warned. "They may rush us now."

Doc grinned evilly. "I'll take care o' them. Watch this."

He turned, looking at each Indian, then, removing his hairpiece and exposing a bald pate beneath it, he turned back and held the hair under each one's nose in turn. As he'd expected, they drew back fearfully. This was almost too much for these superstitious innocents. To cap the performance, Doc drew out his false plates and, holding them between thumb and fingers, snapped them at the Indians. Some of them ran clear out of sight. Only Hoonah Charlie stopped before he'd run to the top of the hill, sensing that this was some trick he might learn from a bigger medicine man. Grinning, he started slowly back toward Doc.

"Mebbe you show Charlie like dat," he suggested.

"Mebbe so," Doc agreed. "Hey Dolf, waddya say we take this big fake down the river with us? No tellin' how many more injuns he's got after your scalp down there. We can't count on 'em all havin' a toothache."

"Sounds good to me. What do you think, Jack?" Dolf asked.

"Why not?" Jack agreed. "It could handle our biggest

worry. With a bunch of miners on the river now, I got a notion Dwan's outfit'll be leary of anything too raw. But that won't stop the injuns. If Charlie'll come, I say let's take 'im along."

Charlie liked the idea real fine. He could feel that good whiskey burning in his stomach. Besides, he wanted to learn from Skookum Doc so he could be even bigger medicine someday among the tribesmen.

CHAPTER 12

OLD John Hedley was well known for a lot of talents, but one of the foremost was being able to cuss. He was cussing now. Seas had been running heavy when they headed north for St. Michael from Unalaska. The water soon rose even more as they plowed northward, making a scant three to four knots against the oncoming swells. Four days and less than four hundred miles northward, the waves became absolutely mountainous. The engine of the small *Idaho*, battling losing odds already, was put at an even greater disadvantage because it had to be idled back rapidly every time they topped a wave, since the stern at such times would rise completely out of the water, exposing the propeller. With loss of water resistance on the propeller, the engine tended to overspeed dangerously if not pulled right back.

Hedley was on the crazily pitching bridge with Cap Magruder when the last straw broke the back of Old John's patience. Word came up from the engineer that they were developing a serious steam leak. The alternatives were to drastically reduce pressure or to risk total loss of power, perhaps even an explosion. Hedley, an old boat-wise veteran of many years in the Missouri River trade, knew what that meant. They could keep up enough speed to give the rudder adequate control, and that was all.

Cap Magruder sized it up. "We'll be losin' headway, actually. Prob'ly could make four or five knots in a dead calm with this much steam. As it is, the current must be running at least eight or ten knots. So we're actually backin' up."

Hedley cursed some more, this time under his breath. He knew they were lucky to have enough headway to simply keep the bow into the waves. If they should lose that and broach, there was a chance of swamping or turning turtle. They'd already been rolling as much as twenty-five or thirty degrees,

114

despite hitting the storm head on. If they turned crosswise to it, the *Idaho* would undoubtedly be lost. So would they.

"If the damn sea goes down a little," Cap said, "I'm gonna risk bringing her around and run back into Unalaska. We can fix the leak there. If it wasn't runnin' so high, I could put out a sea anchor and maybe pull the engine off the line long enough to fix the leak. No way can we rig a sea anchor with a hundred tons o' water bustin' over the bow every time we plow in. We'd better pray the engine doesn't quit altogether."

They literally backed half the way to Unalaska before the seas subsided enough to bring the *Idaho* about and run before them. This misfortune required the better part of three weeks to overcome. Adding the time from Dyea to Unalaska, a frustrating month had gone by for Old John, during which he'd ground his teeth in helpless fury. He didn't reach St. Michael until the day after Quillen's party had started down Lake Bennett, whereas he'd planned to be there at least two weeks before them.

At St. Michael he stood on the pinnacle of frustrated rage, shouting curses at the wind, when he discovered someone had sabotaged his two river steamers. The charred wrecks were beached and burned to the waterline, with much of the irreplaceable machinery heavily damaged. He thought of trying to run the *Idaho* up the Yukon but knew it had too deep a draft.

We'd be hung up on every sand bar, he thought.

His inclination was to fire his whole crew at St. Michael. In most cases it wasn't necessary. They'd heard of the Sky Pilot strike and quit, many heading up on Brown and Shadley's new *River Queen*.

Finally, with no alternative remaining but to get at least some supplies up to his proposed new town before freeze-up, he resolved to patiently pick up the pieces and build at least one boat. It was mid-July before he succeeded in doing this, personally standing guard day and night over the operation. At last, the *Ira Baker*, fully loaded—including deck cargo—

started for the delta on July eighteenth, Old John himself at the wheel. He drove it grimly up the Yukon under full steam, stopping only for wood.

God knows how the boys are makin' out up there without me, he fumed. Or what the hell they think happened to me. Jack sure won't be able to pick out a townsite before I get up there with the stuff to set up a trading post.

Old John had to face the fact that they'd outsmarted themselves. The whole idea of Quillen coming down the river had been to bring with him enough miners to form the nucleus of a successful trading center. Otherwise another season would have got away from them before they could get started. Few miners could have accompanied Hedley in by ship since that was a rich man's route and probably always would be. Now Baker and Hedley were going to lose out to some extent, no matter what John did. Nothing could prevent Brown and Shadley from starting their own settlement once the diggings were located. The first settlement would probably attract the bulk of the miners and keep them there at least awhile.

Besides that, Old John was thinking, I heard that Twead was on the *River Queen*. Whatever else we can say about him, he's a slick businessman. He'll have most of the crew that gets in with Quillen signed up for their winter's supplies on tick. Probably keep 'em in debt to him from now on if he can so they can't switch.

Unpleasant considerations such as these plagued Hedley's brain as he drove relentlessly up the river, carrying dangerously high steam pressure on the boilers the whole distance. "Let the bastards blow up," he cursed. "We're damn near outa the race anyhow. I sure hate to let Ira Baker down like this. But we ain't licked yet by a damn site."

Goldie and his party made good time down the river, although they'd had to run the dogs in ankle-deep water on top of the ice at times. At other times it had been necessary to dodge long open leads forming in the river. They ran out of ice at Lake LaBarge. There he set his men to the task of building a boat. He took no part in the work, lounging in his sleeping robes until noon each day, then perhaps strolling the woods with a gun for a couple of hours. He also kept a supply of whiskey that he, and only he, nipped from time to time. His men knew it from the smell of his breath and resented his selfishness, but said nothing since he paid well. But their loyalty to him was limited. They knew his errand and tolerated him only because they wanted to reach the Sky Pilot diggings among the first. Another source of abrasion was Goldie's insisting that the mushers abandon their dogs. When they refused, he grudgingly allowed them to build a raft to transport the animals.

By June tenth they were as far down as the A.C. Co. Post at Ft. Reliance, where Goldie put ashore to replenish supplies, especially his whiskey. They traded the dogs there for an extra boat. From there on Goldie went slowly, often consulting his map, but concealing it from his companions. After five days of this, he began to suspect, with a rising sense of panic, that something was wrong. None of the landmarks made any sense to him. His temper grew shorter, and he took it out on the others. Finally, wholly exasperated, he announced, "We're gonna have to go back up and start over. Somewhere I missed a key landmark."

Marc LaBrae, one of his mushers, said, "Let us see the map, Goldie. We ain't gonna beat you outa the discovery claims."

Goldie regarded him with hostile suspicion. "No way. I aim to do the navigation. You boys fix' up some harnesses to pull with. We'll have to trail up along the shore. Current's too fast to pole."

"Waddya say, boys," LaBrae said. "Are we gonna take any more guff off this little sneak?"

Goldie sensed what was coming and reached for his pistol, but LaBrae had expected that and knocked him sprawling, grabbing the pistol before Goldie recovered his senses. When he sat up, LaBrae had him covered with his own gun.

"Git the map," LaBrae told Shrimp Todd. "We'll run this show from here in."

They put Goldie and a sufficient amount of supplies for him to survive onto the smaller boat and set him adrift.

"How about a gun?" Goldie yelled back at them.

LaBrae made an obscene gesture in reply. The little con-man was soon out of hearing, becoming a speck on the broad breast of the river. The last he saw of them, his four former employees were bent over his map.

Goldie thought, If what I suspect is so, it won't do them much good. It's a damn fake.

Say what one would for him, Goldie might be destructively avaricious, but he wasn't stupid. He was hoping he'd drift across the *River Queen*, which he knew was on the way up, expecting to meet him, or even one of the A.C. Co. boats. On the other hand, he prayed fervently that Hedley hadn't somehow managed to get his boats built, at least not on time. He knew how he'd fare with Old John.

Prob'ly make me walk the plank, he thought bleakly.

Murphy had joined Dwan after setting fire to Quillen's boats.

"Good work," Dwan had congratulated him. "If the fire got its work in, they'll be a week fixin' them boats at least. But you'd better stay outa sight. Morgette may be over here with blood in his eye. I'll have one of the boys help yuh set up a sorta private camp a few miles down the line. We'll pick yuh up as soon as the ice is out."

It was June tenth—the same day Goldie had reached Ft. Reliance—when Dwan's outfit drifted out and down the lake. They had smooth going, just as Quillen's party would a few days later, until they reached Miles Canyon. The Indians were there with Hoonah Charlie. This was no problem since Hoonah Charlie's brother, Sam, knew Dwan and knew that he worked for "boss man Goldie." So the Indians weren't a source of trouble, but the river was. To keep his lead on Quillen, and since he had skilled boatmen, Dwan decided to risk a run through Miles and White Horse. They made Miles okay, but White Horse cost them a boat, the wreckage of which drifted into the big eddy down below. The boat's occupants all struggled ashore, half-drowned and almost frozen, teeth chattering.

Dwan gathered his group into a camp below the eddy on the east bank, to thaw out the soaked men and sort out recoverable supplies. It was decided that four of the party would have to stay behind and build a raft; otherwise they'd overload the surviving boats. Among these were Turk Haynes, the baldheaded goon who had sweated Jack Quillen in Goldie's cellar, and his squat partner of the slack unshaven jaw and bulging eyes, Blackie Streett. Murphy was another chosen to stay, due to his building skills, and the fourth was Hoonah Charlie's brother, Sam, hired to help man the raft.

"If Morgette and his bunch happen to show up," Dwan said as a parting reminder, "don't pass up any chance to slow them up. But remember, I don't want them women or that kid hurt. Short o' that, yuh can do whatever. But remember, this whole river up above is full o' miners comin' in. They catch yuh in anything too raw and you're gonna stretch rope. There ain't no appeals from their kinda verdicts. So play it safe. Cut their boats loose while they're asleep, sink 'em, drop a few shots near 'em to make 'em nervous. Burn their supplies or boats — but don't hurt them gals, even if they are injuns, or the kid either. Got it? I'll see yuh at the diggins."

After Dwan was out of earshot, Turk looked at Blackie with disgust. "They told me Dwan was tough," he sneered.

"Maybe he is," Blackie said. "Bein' skeered o' stretchin' hemp ain't no sign a man ain't tough. What Rudy said makes sense. I ain't one fer hurtin' no women 'r kids either. All the same, I'd like ta be the man that puts the fatal slug in Dolf Morgette. No miner's meetin' is gonna swing us fer beefin' a gunman. Most likely he makes 'em nervous just bein' around, same as he does us."

* * *

Quillen had a source of expert advice about getting through Miles Canyon and White Horse Rapids—Hoonah Charlie. "Bin troo dat skookum wawa plinty time," Charlie informed him. "Pack round um, let dem damn boat troo all same empty. Catchum down dair." He swept his arm downstream. They spent one day scouting from the banks.

"It sure makes sense to me," Quillen said to Dolf when they got down the eddy below White Horse.

Returning to where they were camped above Miles, Dolf sprained his ankle badly among some loose rocks. "Feels almost like it's busted. Doc'll be able to tell—if I can make it back that far."

He hobbled in with the help of a crutch fashioned from a small spruce.

"Ain't broke," Doc told him. "I'll plaster it up so you don't twist it again. Be okay in a week or so. You'll have to take it easy."

"Helluva time for that," Dolf grumbled.

"Keep ya outa the packin'," Doc grinned.

So Dolf and little Henry were consigned to lounging on some robes in one of the boats, under a canvas sunshade and comfortably behind mosquito netting. Even Jim Too was drafted to carry a pack in the style of Indian dogs.

"By the time we tote all this truck around the rapids," Doc assured Dolf, "you'll be able to navigate. If yuh can't, we'll rig up a stretcher."

Dolf made the best of his predicament, even managing to nap with Henry snuggled next to him. Margaret stayed with them, but Mama helped the men with the packing; like all her kind, she could carry seventy-five pounds, which was as much or more than the average white man—although Thunder and Lightning had no trouble with more than twice that.

Margaret made use of her time relaying supplies some fifty feet up to the top of the knoll above them where they'd first seen the Indians. Turning back from one of these trips, at first she didn't notice Dolf's boat adrift. When she did, it was already in the current some fifty feet from shore and gaining speed.

"Dolf!" she yelled at the top of her voice. "Dolf!"

Her panicky voice roused him from his nap. It took only a second to gain his bearings. He threw off the canvas, despite his sprain, and hobbled to the stern to man the sweep.

He thought, Maybe I can beach her yet. Or swim for it with the kid.

A quick appraisal of his chances at swimming ruled that out. They were already in midstream and riding a rising crest of foamy white water. The banks were almost sheer and as much as twenty or twenty-five feet high.

Can't even beach her now, he thought. We'll have to run it out.

Painfully, he worked forward and brought Henry back, putting him where he could grab him if they capsized. Then he turned to man the sweep. That was when he spotted Margaret sprinting frantically along the cliffs above them. She managed to get slightly ahead of the boat and dove off in a long arc into the raging water. The thought flashed through his mind, This thing is full of submerged rocks. She'll be killed.

He held his breath for what seemed a long time after she'd knifed into the torrent, waiting to see her surface. Finally she did, stroking rapidly to cut them off. Once she was swept into a rock and went under, but came up like a cork, still swimming strongly. He tried to maneuver to her and yet stay away from the rocks. She finally got one hand on the edge of the boat, momentarily lost her grip, then swam alongside and grabbed the edge again, painfully working hand over hand back to where Dolf could help pull her aboard. She was gasping for breath. Dolf found himself breathing almost as hard as Margaret from anxiety for her safety. For a moment she stayed down on her knees in the bottom of the boat, panting; she was not so much weakened from her swim as simply relieved that Henry and Dolf were still alive and with her. Finally she got to her feet.

"You okay?" Dolf asked.

"I'm fine," she gasped. "You give me that oar. I know more about white water than you do."

He was about to protest when he thought, That's probably right. What I know about it is exactly nothing. She's our best bet to pull through alive.

Besides, his ankle hurt like fury, limiting his agility on the sweep oar. He yielded the oar to her, sitting down to hold Henry.

Dolf scanned the water ahead. There was plenty of white water toward both banks, but the volume of water compressed between the enclosed walls had caused the stream to crest at the center. It was obvious that Margaret was cannily seeking to ride this crest, since it would carry them safely over any submerged rocks. Toward the banks were snags of uprooted trees. Others were out in the stream, apt to twist and turn from contact with submerged boulders and threatening to upset the boat.

He turned to watch Margaret's face. She appeared controlled and alert, but unperturbed. Skillfully, she maneuvered them back to the crest after avoiding a tree rolling over in their path. She was getting the feel of the sweep, learning how much to swing it for a given degree of response. The danger, in her opinion, was in losing one's nerve. To an experienced whitewater navigator, this wasn't really too much of a challenge.

After a ten-minute battle, they swung out of the canyon into the rapids. The submerged rocks here made plumes like the windblown manes of horses. Two huge whirlpools shot past on either side of them as Margaret maneuvered between them. To have been caught in either would have meant a long battle to escape and possibly disaster. Once caught, even the experienced could do little with a major whirlpool. She fervently hoped there were no more of them down below. To her intense relief, the worst water seemed to be behind them. White-water rapids appeared more daunting than they actually were. She spotted the big eddy at the foot of the rapids and was maneuvering to land them there well before they reached it. It was the deeper water here that proved their undoing. Margaret couldn't see the large tree turning over in the depths beneath them. Its roots were caught in something on the bottom, and the trunk rose directly under them, turning over the boat without warning. The boat remained next to them upside down, but that was only a partial consolation. Breathing was painfully difficult in water so frigid.

Dolf had grabbed Henry, but holding him above the surface while trying to swim with a cast on his leg was almost impossible. He was completely submerged several times, fighting to keep from inhaling involuntarily under water. Finally, he got one arm on the edge of the boat and literally tossed the baby up on it. He looked frantically around for Margaret, who was not in sight, then tried to scramble out on the boat himself, thinking to scan the water for her from there. While trying to crawl aboard, he saw her pull herself up opposite him. Without a hand from her, he would not have been able to shinny up on the boat.

He lay flat on his stomach for awhile, almost exhausted. After he was sure Margaret and Henry were okay, his next thought was of his weapons. He hoped his .45-90, which was strapped to the gunwhale, and his six-shooters stowed under one of the seats were still with them. He hated to be unarmed at any time, but especially with so many unpredictable threats apt to materialize.

They were able to unmount the sweep oar from its socket and bring it up on top. With it they slowly maneuvered to the bank. Dolf eased into the water again to push the boat firmly ashore and almost sank over his head.

"Bottom's real steep here," he told Margaret.

He hobbled ashore and pulled the bow a foot or two up onto the beach by the mooring rope and tied it. He could see that the rope had been cleanly cut. "Look at this, Maggie," he said.

At this point some unwelcome company made itself known. Turk and Blackie had observed the conclusion of Margaret's battle against the rapids and the boat's final upset. They had run along the bank with the intention of helping, since they'd recently had a similar experience. Then, getting closer, they'd recognized Dolf as he climbed out on the boat's bottom. After that they'd cautiously taken to the brush, moving out of sight up to where the boat was beached.

"What luck," Turk had whispered. "We won't have to finish building our raft after all. We can beef Morgette and get a boat in the bargain."

Blackie was worried about what Turk planned to do with the inevitable witness, Margaret, but was more afraid of his vicious partner, so he thought he'd better not bring that up. He had a notion what Turk would do to her—and the baby, too. He knew Turk didn't like Indians anyhow. When they finally made their presence known, Dolf was standing on the overturned hull, his back to them.

"Well, well, well," Turk announced. "If it ain't my old acquaintance, Dolf Morgette."

Dolf spun around to face the slightly familiar voice. Recognizing the two, he could imagine how they had gotten here, though he hadn't seen either in Dwan's camp. Dolf said nothing. He was calculating his chances of diving into the river and coming up under the boat.

"You got any final prayers," Turk sneered. The typical villain, he had to get in some blow first. Dolf's sudden dive into the river took Turk by surprise. He snapped a hip shot after him from his Winchester but missed widely.

"He's gotta come up somewhere," Turk yelled to Blackie. "You keep the gal covered. I'll get him when he comes up."

Neither realized that the water was so deep directly beneath the boat. Dolf came up into the air pocket trapped inside. He quickly pulled the pin on the hasp holding the hinged lid shut on the seat, then carefully slid his hand in, recovering a pistol. He quickly shoved it in his belt, then retrieved the other. It had been at least thirty seconds since he'd dived into the water.

He heard Turk say, "I musta winged him."

"I didn't see no blood," Blackie said.

Their voices told Dolf their positions. He rose cautiously on the opposite side of the boat and rubbed the water from his eyes.

"Freeze, you two, and drop them guns," he ordered.

They knew the voice and froze. "How do I know you got a gun?" Blackie stalled.

"Turn your head around damn slow and look."

"He's got two guns," Blackie said dismally.

They dropped their guns.

Quillen and his party of packers saw Dolf and Margaret whirl past in the rapids.

"I wonder what the hell happened," Quillen said. "But that gal looks like she knows her onions. I think they'll make it. Let's get down below as fast as we can."

They dropped their packs and started a long footrace. Ave won it, reaching Dolf and Margaret first after a half-hour run. The two Chilkats were close behind. Ave was surprised to see Dolf's prisoners.

"Who're they?" Ave asked.

"The pair that slapped your pa around in Goldie's basement. I reckon he'll be glad to see them."

He told Ave what they'd intended to do to him.

"Why didn't yuh just shoot 'em?" Ave asked practically.

Dolf didn't think it was the time and place to try to explain to Ave that, despite the Morgette reputation, that wasn't really his style. Instead he said, "I expect there's a lot of them other miners comin' down the river a day or so behind us. Thought I'd give one of them miners' meetings your pa puts so much stock in a chance to do its stuff."

They took the two prisoners back up to their camp above the canyon. As Dolf had expected, several boatloads of miners arrived there in the next couple of days. Prominent among them was Stanley King.

Jack Quillen paid a call on him with Dolf along, explaining to Stan that he'd like him to organize a court.

"What for?" King asked, looking suspicious, trying not to mirror his distaste for Dolf.

Jack explained the case.

King said, "It figures you and Morgette would want to get rid of those two. But it's Dolf's word against theirs in this case."

"How about Dolf's wife?" Jack said. "She saw and heard the whole thing."

King almost sneered. "She's injun. The boys won't take no injun's word about anything."

Dolf stifled an urge to punch King in his sanctimonious face.

"She's Chief Henry's daughter, educated back east. Talks better English'n we do," Quillen exploded.

"It don't signify," King said with finality. "You can try some of these other boys, but I don't want anything to do with it. Besides, injuns is injuns."

He knew he'd made a mistake saying it. Dolf's fist crashed into his nose as soon as the words were out. He saw stars; then the back of his head hit the ground and he saw stars again. He didn't try to get up and fight. Some of his party helped him up, eying Dolf resentfully but afraid to say anything. Dolf limped away, disgust plainly registering on his face.

"So that's how the miners' meetings work?" he couldn't help but observe to Jack.

"Not always," Jack protested.

"Once is once too often. I shoulda done what Ave expected me to with these two."

"What was that?"

"Feed 'em to the fish."

Instead he turned them loose with a warning. "Stay outa my way."

Their next several days were occupied by an almost uneventful float through the scenic wilderness down the Yukon and through Lake LaBarge, past the old Hudson's Bay post, Ft. Selkurk, and on to Ft. Reliance, which they reached on the twenty-seventh of June.

CHAPTER 13

DOLF knew that as long as he lived, he would never forget the sight of Margaret arrowing off the cliff into the deadly unknown depths of Miles Canyon to save the lives of those she loved. Undoubtedly she had. He probably would have clumsily upset the boat, drowning them both.

As they continued down the river, he welcomed every opportunity to show her his gratitude, sometimes simply squeezing her hand or touching her and smiling with a look in his eyes she understood.

After supper one evening, with Henry safely in the charge of Mama, they strolled along the Yukon to be alone for a while. Dolf put his arm around her and they walked close together, watching the mighty river sweep past and thrilling to the awesome stillness and solitude. The land was suffused with color—purple lupine, fireweed, and wild roses—while aspen, willow, and poplar crowded down to the water's edge from the higher hills, which were crowned largely with spruce and pine.

"I owe you my life, again," Dolf whispered, stooping to kiss her gently.

She held him fiercely. "You and our son are my life. I saved *my own life*."

Dolf had never been so much in love with this small contradictory bundle of fire and tenderness. He held her close for a long while, gently bestowing light kisses on her face, cradling her head between his hands. Suddenly she opened her eyes and grinned mischievously.

"All of a sudden I feel sleepy, Dolf. Let's go up and go to bed."

"Funny thing," Dolf said. "Me too. Besides, the mosquitoes are bad—we can get away from them in our tent."

He prayed that their life would never change, but the past had touched him with too many bitter experiences. Enjoy it now! he told himself. I'll make this last if it's in my power. And Lord, how I'll try to do my best for Maggie and the kid!

Goldie had never met Forrest Twead, but he'd been instructed that Twead would be boss when he reached the Yukon. He was just about to have a very bad two weeks in his company. He saw the *River Queen*'s smoke far downstream and maneuvered his boat to be picked up by it.

Twead had been expecting Goldie or Dwan to send him a guide.

"So you're Goldie Smith?" Twead observed, not offering to shake hands. "Who the hell d'ya leave in charge up above?"

"Nobody," Goldie blurted, nonplussed. He told his hard-luck story.

"What a damned fool stunt. Don't you know how to handle men?" Twead managed them in exactly the same unfeeling way as he was now managing Goldie, but this completely escaped him. Then, after they'd talked some more, he said, "What makes you think the map's a fake?"

"Couldn't make head'r tail of it."

"Jeezuz!" was all Twead said. He had his own copy of it. He had the *River Queen* retrace Goldie's route after stopping at Ft. Reliance for possible news of either Dwan or Quillen.

It took Twead just two days to locate the stream that, from the map, he was satisfied was the Sky Pilot. "All the landmarks check," he chided Goldie sarcastically. "I don't see how the hell you missed."

The *River Queen* carried a load of prospectors who had wintered at St. Michael. They swarmed ashore now, some starting upstream without even unloading the bulk of their supplies. Goldie knew that Brown and Shadley weren't interested in the gold, only the commercial exploitation of the miners. He sadly watched his own chance of making the big strike first go out the window. He wasn't the kind to brave the bush alone. But a new idea possessed him. He was planning to lay out a townsite at the right moment. He and Twead, Captain Barlow, Swede Larson the engineer, and a chink cook and two old salts with no taste for land were the only people left on board.

"We'll soon know if we've struck it," Twead said. "If we have, we start building the trading post."

Goldie had other ideas. He had already developed a great distaste for Twead, dating from their first meeting. They were too much alike. Twead can build his own damn trading post, Goldie thought.

The first reports from upstream were not encouraging. One early returnee reported disgustedly, "Maybe ten cents a pan. Can hit that in almost any stream up here." Later reports were no better; the best showing was two bits a pan. It wasn't enough to buy beans, and everyone knew it. After ten days the bulk of disappointed prospectors who had run out of provisions started filtering back in an ugly mood. The implications were fairly obvious to Twead. He told Goldie, "If this map really is a fake, we're in for trouble. I've got a notion to pull out for Ft. Reliance and wait'll Quillen shows up."

"Thanks ta yer map, he may never show up," Goldie growled.

Twead understood all too well what the other meant. He had a sinking feeling in his stomach over the possibility that Dwan's thugs may have killed Quillen since they thought the map rendered him unnecessary.

"Not only that," Goldie delighted in informing him, "but if ya strand these boys, you'll never operate up here again. Yer gonna have to stay an' face the music." How he loved to tell Twead that and watch his weaselish expression. But Twead knew men. He began to circulate among the disgruntled returnees, grousing about how Brown and Shadley had been victimized themselves by what may have been a fake map planted by Baker and Hedley.

"We're in this thing together, boys. If it fizzles out, the supplies and transportation are on us." He didn't know how

Brown and Shadley would feel about that, but if it saved his own neck he didn't care.

"Besides," he argued, "we know Jack Quillen knows for sure where the Sky Pilot is, and he's due down here any day. The party's on Brown and Shadley up till then at least. If we do make the big strike, you can all charge your winter supplies with B and S."

For the time being, this held off a lynching with him as the guest of honor. The arrival of Dwan with Goldie's plug-uglies brightened the picture a little for Twead. It brightened it even more for Goldie, who knew he could control at least them.

"You got any idea where Quillen is?" Goldie asked Dwan.

"Not the slightest. If my boys did their job, he could be anywhere."

"Dead?" Twead asked ominously.

"Not likely. I just told 'em to slow 'em down, except Morgette—his case don't matter."

"Well, the sooner Quillen gets here now, the better. Some of the boys are still prospecting the side creeks, but I think we've been tricked."

"Why don't we go up and meet Quillen and bring him down on the *River Queen* in style?" Goldie jibed slyly and earned a poisonous look from Twead.

By the time Quillen, Dolf, and party reached Ft. Reliance, the A.C. Company's *Bertha*, out of St. Michael, was tied up there. As a result they soon learned that Hedley wouldn't be up the Yukon very soon. The *Bertha*'s captain told them what had happened.

"Old John was cussin' one o' them boats back in shape when we pulled out. He'll be up here all right, but God knows when. You'll hear him at least a hundred miles away still cussin'. Prob'ly be at least a month yet."

"Well," Jack said when he was alone with Dolf and Doc, "this calls for a leetle powwow. As I see it, we're right between a rock and a hard spot. We got a responsibility to Baker and Hedley—no denyin' that—but I got a personal responsibility to all the boys that're comin' in here on my say-so. According to McQuesten up at the A.C. Co. store, there's even a raft of 'em on the *River Queen*." He laughed at a sudden thought. "By now they know they're barkin' up the wrong creek. Maybe they've hung Twead an' Goldie 'n' Dwan. I hope so. But if *I* keep 'em standin' around on one foot for a month waitin' on Old John to *maybe* get here, they'll hang me—and there won't be no maybe about that."

They decided their only choice was to go in to the Sky Pilot. For the first time, Jack drew a true map for the others. "Here's my idea of how we outsmart Brown and Shadley in spite of our steamboats gettin' burned. We cut over the ridge from about where I'd guess the *River Queen* is tied up right now. There'll be at least fifty other honest prospectors follerin' us, so I ain't afraid we'll get cut out of the discovery claims—it's the unwritten law up here. What I'm countin' on is no one knowin' the best place for a trading post is really down the Sky Pilot where it hits the Yukon. I'm hopin' Twead and Goldie set up business right where they are. That's where our trail will start over the ridge. When Old John gets here, we'll set up our own post in the choice spot, right above the mouth of the Sky Pilot itself."

As an old-timer, Jack Quillen was personally known to almost every one of the miners who had come up on the *River Queen*, as well as those coming down the Yukon a few days behind him. The same could be said for the couple dozen that followed him down to the *River Queen* from around Ft. Reliance. There was no possibility of foul play from Twead's associates with all of them along.

Dolf thought, Probably even I'm safe just now.

But he was always on the alert anyhow. And he saw no reason not to take Margaret and Henry along. Safer now than comin' down the river, he reasoned.

* * *

Quillen's arrival at the *River Queen* caused a near riot for a few moments.

"Keep yer shirts on," he yelled. "I'm callin' for a miners' meeting right here and now to organize the Sky Pilot district. Till we get some articles on paper, I ain't budgin'."

That gained immediate compliance. With no dissent, he was able to establish his own rules, which were little different from those universally accepted in the north.

"Now," he said, "we need a recorder and judge for the district." He thought his problem there would be solved, since he'd seen Stan King's party arrive in the midst of the proceedings. "You all know Stan King. I nominate him as recorder and judge of the new Sky Pilot district." This selection was universally acclaimed.

"How about a sheriff?" someone asked.

Twead, who was present but had kept out of the rule making, shouted, "I nominate Rudy Dwan. He's a good man—I've known him for years."

Dolf hadn't seen Dwan in evidence, but assumed he was around. Dwan, in fact, had had a few days to canvas for the job. In addition, most of this group were already on Twead's books for their winter's supplies.

Quillen was ready to explode when Dolf, recognizing it, nudged him. "Let Rudy have the job," Dolf said in a low voice. "I don't need it to do what you want me for—in fact, I don't want it. Especially not with King as judge. We'd never be able to work together. Besides, you'll have your own settlement in a few weeks. Get me elected up there."

Quillen didn't want to accept that, but recognized the sense of it. "Okay," he agreed reluctantly. "If Dwan is what I think he is, this crowd'll get rid of him themselves if need be. He'll soon discover this ain't Montana."

"Any beefs against Dwan as sheriff?" Stan King inquired, already asserting his new-felt importance. He particularly eyed Jack Quillen.

"He suits us," Jack said.

This easy agreement obviously puzzled both King and Twead.

"Now," Quillen yelled so everyone could hear him. "Let's wait'll morning and get an early start. That moose pasture is big enough for all of us and plenty more, and it ain't goin' away if we all get some rest. It's a long trek over there."

The next day Jack led the group, now consisting of perhaps one hundred prospectors, across the ridge to the west. They plunged on all day till almost midnight, since the sun remained up nearly twenty-four hours in June—except for a few minutes on either side of midnight. Once on the Sky Pilot, Jack located "discovery" and "one above," helping Ave stake "one below." Then the prospectors drew ballots prepared by King for other claims. Few of them slept; most headed up or down the creek at once, roughly locating their claims.

"I'm hopin' no one heads for the mouth of the river," Jack said. "They might start thinkin' and say somethin' that got back to Twead. Our chance of winning all the marbles back will be that townsite. Dern site easier tradin' down there than over that ridge—and quicker, especially in winter."

In the next days some of the miners began to hit four or five dollars to a pan, figuring the standard rate of $17.50 an ounce. But most were busy setting up sluice boxes. After the placer gold was cleaned up, the arctic system of shafting down to bedrock would commence. This system consisted of laboriously melting through the permafrost with fires, scooping out perhaps a foot a day. Once down in paying gravel, it would be brought to the surface and sluiced. When winter froze up the available water, piles of pay dirt were built up to be sluiced in the spring—a system known as spring cleanup.

Even Twead and Goldie had joined the stampede to file claims, then returned to start their settlement. They named it Brownley, a composite of Brown's and Shadley's names. The rich returns over at the diggings had set Goldie to gloating. To Dwan he exulted, "Well, Sheriff, come next summer there'll be a million in gold shipped outa here if I don't get it all in my joint before then."

"Better go easy at first," Dwan advised. "I'm supposed to be keepin' things square. Let's not queer the deal by gettin' too raw right away."

"I know my business," Goldie assured him. One aspect of his business that surprised everyone was the arrival from upstream of five dance-hall girls. They created quite a stir until Old John pulled in with the *Ira Baker* on August first. By then Brownley was shaping up as a fair-sized settlement, dominated by the B & S Mercantile and Goldie's Skookum Two saloon.

"Passed the *River Queen* goin' back for another load," Hedley told Jack Quillen. "As soon as these prospectors get unloaded, we'll drop down to yore townsite, unload this scow, and I'm gonna do the same thing if I can beat the freeze up."

The *Ira Baker*'s departure not four hours after its arrival at Brownley created a great deal of speculation, particularly on Twead's part. "Now what do you suppose that old bastard's up to?" he asked Goldie.

"Damfino," Goldie said. "But if I was you, I'd find out."

CHAPTER 14

JACK Quillen had selected an ideal location for their trading post on a bend in the Sky Pilot River about two miles above the Yukon. A small tributary provided ideal shelter for wintering a steamboat; spring breakup would be mild there compared to the Sky Pilot itself or the Yukon.

"Good, good," Hedley observed. " 'Cause I plan to winter here. There'll be a hundred boys lookin' for passage out after spring cleanup. Some of 'em been up here ten years tryin' to make a big stake and go home. We'll pay for this scow on that one trip."

Dolf and Doc weren't planning to work claims, although they'd both filed on them. Stanley King had objected to Indians filing claims and had carried his point, which had left out Thunder and Lightning. As a result, Doc and Dolf worked out an agreement with them on shares.

"I aim to take a vacation," Doc said. "Got a few hundred books I've been aimin' to read if Old John brought 'em up here. How about you, Dolf?"

"I dunno. Doesn't look like keepin' the peace is gonna be any problem. I might do some hunting and trapping. And read some of them books of yours if I don't need a dictionary to get through too many of 'em."

Hedley instructed Quillen regarding what he wanted built, supervised the unloading of supplies and their storage under canvas, then made off down the Yukon at top speed in the *Ira Baker*.

Dolf and Doc set about building adjoining cabins near the post store, which was rising under Jack's supervision. Ave helped, and they hired some Nenana Indians to speed up the work.

Quillen's first customers were from a group of prospectors Old John had brought up on the *Ira Baker*. Jack had also cir-

136

culated word up at the diggings and a few others had dropped down, some just to look the place over. These visitors conveyed the first hint of dissatisfaction over what was going on up at Goldie's place in Brownley. "Just like in Juneau," one of them observed. "Them gals attract the boys over for a little fun, and they come back with empty pokes and sometimes a lump on their head."

"How about the sheriff—don't he put a stop to that?" Jack asked slyly.

"Hell, he lives at the Skookum!"

"Why don't you ask the judge to step in?"

The fellow snorted. "Twead's got old King right in the palm of his hand. I'm thinkin' we may have to clean that gang out someday."

"You're right," Quillen stated emphatically. "*You're* gonna hafta clean them out. *You* put 'em in. *I* was gonna suggest Morgette for sheriff."

"Why the hell didn't you?"

"Would you have voted for him?"

The man avoided answering. "I sure as hell would now," he said.

"Too late," Jack said. "Do your trading over here. We ain't havin' any trouble, and we won't. Spread the word. We're offering credit on supplies, too, if anyone needs it. I don't expect anyone will unless they keep losin' their pokes over at Goldie's, or unless it's someone just comin' in to the diggins. Anyhow, spread the word."

Gradually business began to pick up, either because it was easier traveling to Baker and Hedley's store, or because the boys were avoiding Brownley to keep from being robbed.

It hadn't taken Twead long to unravel the puzzle of where the *Ira Baker* had gone after its brief stop. However, he didn't yet know enough about the local geography to appreciate the threat of Quillen's strategic location. By the time he did, a month had passed and Goldie's almost-completed Skookum

Two was aggravating the problem. Twead felt he'd better take it up with the source of the trouble. He imperiously sent for Goldie.

"Tell him to go to hell," Goldie told Twead's messenger.

Dwan and Goldie were at a table in the partially completed barroom. Goldie had already sounded out the sheriff regarding his allegiance.

"Hell, I don't like Twead worth a cent," said Dwan. "Never did. Wouldn't have come up here in the first place if it wasn't for that bad break."

"You still expectin' trouble with Morgette over that?"

Dwan had thought about that awhile. "I dunno. He's a funny duck. I don't think he'll make a move unless he can prove I killed Harvey Parrent—and he can't because I didn't."

"Who did?" Goldie had asked.

"I don't know. But I got my suspicions about who mighta put someone up to it."

"Who?"

"I ain't sayin' till I got some proof." But he was thinking, and not for the first time, Twead was all-fired anxious to get me up here. He knew I wouldn't leave Ft. Belton, though, unless I had to. He's just slick enough to have figured out a surefire way to make me anxious to leave. He knew nobody in their right mind would face Morgette and that Morgette would sure as hell suspect me—everyone else did.

It was at this point that Twead walked over to the table. Without preamble he announced to Goldie, "You're fired."

"No, I ain't," Goldie retorted. "I done quit early this mornin'—I just didn't get around to tellin' you yet."

"Either way suits me," Twead said. "But there's somethin' we ought to talk over, and it's this. Business is falling off."

"Maybe for you," Goldie said smugly, blowing cigar smoke at Twead.

"It will for you damn soon if it hasn't already. The reason is the way you run this place. The boys over on the Sky Pilot are catching onto you."

"Let 'em. I got the only gals for a thousand miles except for klootches, and who the hell can stand the smell of a squaw? The boys'll keep comin'."

Seeing himself at a dead end with Goldie, Twead turned to Dwan. "I want you as sheriff to do something about this den of iniquity. Don't forget you're still workin' for the company."

"Was," Dwan informed him. "I quit this A.M., too." As a matter of fact, the event had occurred just as Goldie had passed him five thousand dollars in greenbacks.

"I don't give a damn whether you work for the company or not; you've got a job to keep this place safe!" Twead exploded.

Dwan smiled contemptuously.

"Safe?" he asked. "I feel safe. How about you, Goldie?"

"Never felt safer."

They were both laughing when Twead stomped out in a rage. They stopped laughing when the *River Queen* returned and Twead started to load Brown & Shadley merchandise on board, rather than unloading more. Goldie moseyed over to see what was going on.

"I'm pullin' out," Twead told him.

"You can't do that," Goldie protested.

"The hell I can't!"

At this point Goldie pulled out his six-shooter, only to put it away quickly when he felt a Winchester poking his spine.

As Goldie was leaving, Twead said, "Before you or Dwan come over here with any of those thugs and try to stop me, look around. I got a dozen men over here just like this one, waitin' with Winchesters."

Goldie changed tactics. "Where the hell are yuh goin'?"

"None of your damned business."

And by morning he was gone. To add insult to injury, he'd torched his building, almost burning down the Skookum Two as well before the fire subsided.

Twead had been over earlier to make a deal with Quillen for a lot and had been made to pay through the nose.

"Hell, I can't stop him," Jack told Dolf afterward.

McQuesten says he's movin' the A.C. store down in the spring. Might as well make some money off of 'em. If I'm any judge, there'll be plenty of business for all of us here by next year."

"Where d'ya suppose Goldie'll go?" Dolf mused.

"Stay there till spring. If he tries to come over here, we'll run him outa the country. I'm gonna get up a new election and make you sheriff."

"I don't want the job," Dolf announced, emphatically. "I'm set for a peaceful winter. So's this community. You don't need me. If you ever do need me, have the sheriff, whoever you pick, deputize me."

"You got any suggestions for the job?" asked Quillen, almost angrily.

"*I* have," Doc said. He'd heard how Marc LaBrae had taken Goldie's boat, so he told Quillen. "Him and them other three been dodgin' Goldie ever since, but they got claims up the river. I think LaBrae's your man."

By a word-of-mouth campaign, Quillen and Stanley King were able to have Dwan supplanted as sheriff of the Sky Pilot District by Marc LaBrae. A delegation was sent over to give Dwan the word. Goldie liked it even less than Rudy did.

When Old John returned, running nip and tuck against freeze-up, he was greatly pleased at the way things were working out — all except Twead's moving in on them.

"Hell," he snorted, "he's worse'n Dwan and Goldie. If he operates here like he did in Ft. Belton, I'll burn him out. Oughta burn the *River Queen* at least just to even the score for mine."

CHAPTER 15

DOLF and his family were snugly settled in their cabin when the first snow fell. By then the woodpile, gotten up for them by several Nenana choppers, was almost mountainous. In fact, woodpiles were one of the most prominent features of St. John, as Quillen had whimsically named the growing village, after Hedley.

Among the mail brought up on the *Ira Baker* were several letters for Dolf. He eagerly read those from his family, but saved a bulky, official-looking envelope from Washington, D.C., till last. He was almost afraid to open it, half-expecting a summons to an extradition hearing over his Canadian misadventure.

There was a second sealed envelope inside the first, wrapped in a covering letter. He was surprised at the signature on the cover letter. It was Alby Gould's. He recalled the last time he'd seen Alby, in Pinebluff. He could still vividly recall the lamplight haloing Victoria Wheat's hair as she'd impulsively kissed Alby—the scene Dolf had tragically misinterpreted, if he could believe her letter. He still had it, but hadn't answered it. *I suppose I oughta try,* he thought. *By now she must have heard about Margaret. I wonder what she thinks of me now?*

Alby Gould's letter read:

Dear Dolf:

So you'll understand why I'm writing to you, Ira Baker has written me several times regarding the events of the past year in Montana and in Alaska. As a member of the Northwest Stockgrowers Association, I've known Ira Baker and John Hedley for years. I particularly repose great trust in Baker's integrity and judgment.

Due chiefly to his testimony, I, as a member of the U.S. Senate from my home state, have made extensive inquiries into the sub rosa efforts of various interests to secure the ex-

tradition of those persons associated with Gabriel Dufan, your-self included. My conclusion has been that such efforts are ill-advised and unjustified. The prejudices of some agencies up north, and their readiness to consider all U.S. cowmen as largely rustlers and gunmen, are well known. Illegal incursions into the U.S. of parties from up there, of a similar nature to Dufan's and perhaps less justified by altruistic motives, are not unknown.

To shorten a long story, I have been able to convince the U.S. Marshal's office here that, far from serving the nation's interest by apprehending any U.S. citizens for extradition—particularly you—it is to our advantage, in view of your present whereabouts and the well-known lawless conditions there, to tender you the enclosed commission, which you will find self-explanatory.

I was asked by our mutual friend, Victoria Wheat, who is now residing here in Washington, to convey her best wishes to you and congratulate you on your recent marriage and addition to the family. She was wondering if you had ever received her letter posted to you at Ft. Belton.

> *I remain sincerely,*
> *Your friend,*
> *Alby Gould*

Dolf considered the many things the letter implied but had cleverly left unsaid, such as that perhaps the R.N.W.C.M.P. may not have been above entering the U.S. unofficially themselves. Or that Alby realized Hedley was more prone to rashness than his partner. And especially that Victoria Wheat now recognized Dolf's situation, whether she was happy about it or not. He wondered what her residence in the same place as Alby Gould might imply. But he was not remorseful. His feeling for Margaret was absolutely certain in his mind. But I should write to Victoria anyhow, he thought.

He gingerly opened the other envelope and was most astounded, despite Alby's remarks, at what was enclosed—a commission as U.S. deputy marshal for the Yukon District of

...e Territory of Alaska. An oath of office to be executed and ...n acceptance form were also enclosed, to be returned as soon ...s possible.

Old John Hedley carried some other explosive information ...r Dolf, to be given to him at Hedley's discretion as to the ...roper time, if ever. It was contained in a letter from Ira ...aker, the pertinent excerpt reading:

A hardcase here in Montana has confessed to killing Harvey ...arrent for hire, just prior to his being hanged legally. ...lthough it hasn't yet become public, I have discovered from ...eliable sources that he confessed in a sworn statement that ...orrest Twead paid him to do it. Twead's motive was un- ...oubtedly twofold; he knew that Brown and Shadley want to ...rab all the land around here, and he knew that Dwan would ...e suspected if Parrent were killed, and would therefore be ...villing to go to Alaska, which he was reluctant to do before ...hen. I'm sure Brown and Shadley know the facts as well as I ...lo and may warn Twead. That's probably impossible before ...pring; at least I hope so.

I am aware that Dolf Morgette is being made U.S. deputy ...narshal up there. If, in your opinion, he will arrest Twead ...nd bring him out for trial, give him this information. If not, ...t is neither in his best interest nor ours to have him simply ...commit a revenge killing. I personally doubt, despite his ...eputation, that he is capable of that.

Hedley decided to keep this to himself for a while, regard-...ess. Besides, proper papers were needed to legally apprehend Twead—unobtainable before the next year. And the village of St. John did not have a jail.

Dolf had Old John, as notary, swear him into office as deputy U.S. marshal. The matter of sending the acceptance would have to wait for spring thaw.

"Well, Marshal," Hedley said, not really being serious, "waddya aim to do about that blot on the scenery Goldie's runnin'?"

"Not a damn thing," Dolf said, realizing Hedley's mood.

"The miners keep it goin'. If they wanta shut it down, all they gotta do is stop goin' over there. My first official act is gonna be to go over to my cabin and eat."

As he left, Old John was grinning inwardly: Good thinking. If we shut 'em down over there, they'd prob'ly try to come over here. But I'm gonna have to send their mail over there somehow.

When Dolf reached his cabin he gave Margaret a kiss and went right over to inspect what was cooking on the stove.

"If your mustache is frozen again," said Margaret, "get your long curious nose outa that pot. You remind me of father."

"Good," Dolf said. "Him and Abe Lincoln were my two heroes."

After eating, Dolf got out his writing materials and went to work. Letters home and a thank-you to Alby Gould presented no problem. Victoria Wheat was a different proposition. He made several unsatisfactory starts, crushing them up and tossing them into the flames of the fireplace.

"What in the world are you trying to write?" Margaret finally asked, noticing his trouble.

Dolf saw no reason to be evasive; he knew his heart. "Writin' an old flame to give her the sad news that you beat her time."

"You want me to help?" Margaret asked. But her inner feeling was not truly as humorous as she made it sound. Dolf didn't notice that. If he had been watching her face, perhaps he would have.

"She's really only a friend. Victoria Wheat. While I was laid up at their home, she confessed to a schoolgirl crush she used to have on me. I suspect she's getting ready to be hitched to Alby Gould."

He'd already innocently allowed Margaret to read Alby's letter. His reference to Victoria Wheat in it had caused Margaret a pang near her heart. Her experiences as an Indian, an intruder in the white community outside the school at Carlisle, had left her with an unavoidable sense of inferiority around most whites. Above all, somewhere deep inside, she felt she could never be good enough for Dolf. When he'd had to knock down Stanley King because of her, she'd thought, Will it always be this way? Will he always have to fight to have me accepted?

She knew that no matter how much he might cow others into outward acceptance because they feared him, they would never really change inwardly. If it's like this up here among these rough men, she asked herself, what will it be like if he takes me home among his own people? Suppose his family rejects me?

Dolf tossed his latest unsatisfactory effort carelessly at the fireplace, not noticing that he missed his mark. It came to rest beside on the hearth. Disgusted, he rose, leaving everything where it was, and said, "I'm gonna mosey over to Doc's for a while and tackle this later. I need some more books anyhow. Wanna bring Henry and come along?"

"No, you go ahead. I don't want to wake Henry up. I'll keep him and Mama company."

He kissed her lightly, slipped on a sweater for the short jaunt outside, and left.

Margaret fought a losing battle with her curiosity, but she was a woman—moreover, one with fearful suspicions. She'd seen Dolf rereading Victoria's letter many times, looking ever so sad, puzzling over how to answer it, and she had wrongly suspected what the problem might be. His real problem had been how to avoid needlessly hurting Victoria. Margaret was not as sure of Dolf's love for her as he was.

Margaret tremulously picked up Victoria's letter, hating herself, yet knowing what she must find out. The first words, "My darling Dolf," pierced her heart like a deadly dagger. No woman wrote in this fashion unless there had been much between her and a man. Tears clouded her eyes, and there was a tight numbing pain in her chest. She could hardly read the rest, seeing it through a blur. As she read, she understood everything about his leaving Pinebluff. Otherwise he would never have accepted me, she thought. Victoria's words—"Dolf, I love you deeply. . . . I will be waiting for you, and waiting for a letter even before you come *home*"—absolutely shattered Margaret's happy little world. She had seen Victoria Wheat, a radiant goddess who was everything an Indian girl, convinced of her inferiority and lack of worth, could never hope to be. She couldn't see how Dolf could possibly want a little, dusky mouse when such an angel could be his. Yet she loved him so, realizing all the same that it was not *her* love that mattered. From that moment, she knew in her heart that she must release him no matter how much it hurt her. Her only surviving hope was perhaps in his crushed-up letter on the hearth.

Its first words momentarily raised her spirits.

He had written only "Dear Victoria" as the salutation, all quite proper. Then she read: "I got your letter and have kept it. I didn't know exactly what to say. As you know I am married. I can't deny that I felt the same way about you. But there is never any going back in this world whether we'd *like to* or not. . . ." There he had given it up, with no mention of being in love with his wife. She thought, He could at least have said, "I am married *and happy*." But he didn't.

She threw his crumpled letter in the fire, rearranged his writing things like they had been, and went into the bedroom, where she threw herself face down on their bed and sobbed like a broken-hearted child. Jim Too, who had been snoozing near Henry's cradle, came over and licked her face in a puzzled effort to console her. She placed a grateful hand on his head and patted him.

I can't let Dolf know, she thought. The right time will be in the spring when I can leave. She began to hate the knowledge that she was carrying another child. She'd meant to tell Dolf soon and share the great happiness she'd expected that might bring him. Instead she hoped that she and it would die somehow. She resolved to put off telling him as long as possible.

CHAPTER 16

MAIL service was an uncertain proposition along the Yukon and would be until after the turn of the century when John Clum would organize it. Hedley was ex-officio postmaster at the Sky Pilot, primarily because the *Ira Baker* had brought in the last batch of mail, arriving about a week behind the *River Queen*. Both of the steamboats were now frozen in for the winter in Squaw Creek, across from St. John.

Letters along the Yukon were, by custom, carried by anyone and everyone, sometimes almost worn out in transit. The custom was for the recipient to pay one dollar for each letter, unless he couldn't afford to. Bearers of letters were always as welcome as a spring thaw.

Because he wanted Ave Quillen to make a little money, Hedley appointed him to carry the mail over to Goldie's place by dog team, a two-day round trip. Snow was threatening when Ave departed, but even the worst blizzard was no problem for an experienced man. No one anticipated trouble on an errand such as that, even from a cutthroat crew like Goldie's. Outside of their trade, most of them were as sentimental and soft-hearted as young girls.

It was snowing heavily when Ave reached the former settlement of Brownley, which Goldie had snidely renamed for himself: Goldley. Ave was chilled from the slash of the wind and snow driving into his face, so he welcomed the thought of reaching the warmth of the Skookum Two. But he had no intention of hanging around a place like that for the night. He left his dog team hitched, planning to siwash it somewhere up on the ridge.

Ave was scarcely prepared to find things going full blast inside, but he stumbled into a rowdy half-drunk crowd with dancing and games going on in the back room. He didn't quite know how to announce his errand. Dwan's was the first familiar face he saw. Dwan was standing near the front of the bar, downing a shot of whiskey. Ave didn't trust him, but he had no reason to fear him under the circumstances. Dwan spotted him and appeared a little surprised.

"Mr. Dwan," Ave said. "I brought over the mail off the boat." He held up the mail sack.

Dwan was half-drunk—had been since he'd lost his job as sheriff and fallen out of Goldie's favor. He wanted to go back to Ft. Belton but morosely faced the fact that he couldn't until spring, if then. The only money he had was what was left of the five-thousand-dollar bribe from Goldie, and he'd blown half that already on cards and the girls. The thought of going out and working his claim didn't appeal to him much. But he knew he'd better get away from there before he dribbled his money all away or, worse yet, Goldie had him rolled. He'd been turning these black prospects over sourly in his mind when Ave came in.

"Mail," Dwan yelled. That got everyone's attention as he knew it would.

"How should I pass it out?" Ave asked Rudy, puzzled.

"Hell, kid, just dump it out on the floor and let everyone sort out their own."

He grabbed the bag and did it himself. There was a lot of shuffling and jostling, even the girls getting mixed up in the press. Dwan watched with amused detachment, finally wading in at the tail end and retrieving a couple of fat envelopes. He returned to the bar. Ave was standing there awkwardly, wondering how to collect his money.

"You look half-froze, kid," Rudy said. "Let me buy you a drink."

"I almost never had one before," Ave admitted.

"Do yuh good. Here." Rudy got him a shot. The tall youth almost strangled on it but got it down.

"Thanks," he wheezed. "I think."

Rudy laughed and slapped him on the back. "How about another one?"

"No thanks. As soon as I get my money, I gotta go."

"What money?" Dwan asked.

Ave explained the custom to him.

"Hey, boys," Dwan yelled. "We owe the kid a buck a letter. Custom o' the country."

He shelled out his two dollars and passed them to Ave. Others began to come and do the same. As starved as most were for word from outside, they'd have probably been glad to pay five dollars, with a couple of exceptions.

Turk Haynes was one of them. Drunk—and ugly even when he wasn't—he snarled, "Why the hell should I pay this string bean a buck fer what costs two cents everywhere in the U.S.? This is the U.S., ain't it? There's a stamp on this letter, ain't there?" He held it up for everyone to see.

Dwan stuck in his oar, feeling sorry for Ave, who looked embarrassed. "Look, Turk," Rudy said. "It's a custom up here. This kid's come fifty miles through a blizzard with them letters."

"Ta hell with blizzards," Turk growled. He turned back to the bar, ignoring them both.

"Here, kid," Dwan said. "I'll pay his dollar."

Turk heard him and swung his head around, getting red in the face. "You ain't payin' my buck. I don't owe no buck." He came swaying over to confront them. "Nobody owes him no buck." He back-handed Ave in the chest. "Yuh oughta give that dough back to all these here people."

The crowd stood around, embarrassed. Most were afraid to challenge Turk, especially with his big-eyed buddy Blackie Streett at the bar, ready to back him.

"Hand it over," Turk demanded of Ave, shoving him hard.

Ave stumbled away, afraid, but not willing to be robbed either. He'd never had a serious fight with a man, although he'd wrestled the Indian boys. He didn't know what to do.

Turk pushed him again, and he swung a wild haymaker at the big gorilla. To Ave's amazement, he knocked Turk to his knees, stunned. He stayed down a moment, shaking his head, then rose unsteadily, assuming a boxing stance.

"Okay, kid. You asked for it."

"Hold it, Turk," Dwan warned.

Turk swung his head toward him. "You want some, too?"

"It ain't my game, Turk. This is," he added, pulling a six-shooter. "Git outside, kid." As Rudy followed him through the door, a shot blasted into his back, sending him sprawling on his face. He managed to roll over as Blackie Streett came out the door, smoking pistol in his hand. Blackie had just time enough to be surprised that Rudy was still able to point a six-shooter at him; then he felt the .45 slug plow into his gut. He fell right in the door.

"Next sonofabitch out gets the same," Dwan yelled with tremendous effort. He staggered to his feet and managed to get to Ave's sled. "I'm hit bad, kid. Try ta get me outa here—they'll be after us." He collapsed into the sled.

Ave was startled by these swift happenings, but not really scared. It had happened too quickly. He swiftly untied the dogs and urged them into a run, unslinging his .45-90 to cover their retreat. Turk ran out, saw this, and just as quickly ducked back inside. Ave triggered a warning shot, but aimed away from the building, where he realized there were innocent people. No one else was brave enough to venture out before the driving snow blotted them from view.

"Anybody back there got dogs?" Ave yelled at the barely conscious Dwan. Dwan shook his head. "They won't catch us then," Ave declared. He stopped briefly to put on his snowshoes, then ran the dogs for a couple of miles, before stopping again to examine Rudy. He tightly tied up his wound the best way he could. As best Ave could tell, he'd been shot in the left shoulder blade with the bullet glancing up through the heavy part of his arm. He managed to bundle Rudy into blankets and a sleeping robe, then mushed rapidly onward.

The only thought in Ave's mind was to get Dwan to Skookum Doc as soon as he could; he was good for the hundred-mile round trip if the dogs were.

Doc examined Dwan on the kitchen table in his cabin.

"Tore hell outa him," Doc said, "but the bullet ain't in him. If he don't get infected, he'll be as good as new in a month."

Doc cleaned the wounds, stitched up the exterior rips in him, and put him in bed under an opiate.

"I never thought I'd be tucking this one in my bed," Doc shrugged. He looked apologetically at Dolf. "I hate to ask you, but we're gonna need a nurse occasionally, especially if I have to run up to the diggins if some damn fool needs me. You know who the best one around is, I guess."

Dolf nodded. Hedley, who was present, figured it was time to tell Dolf that Dwan hadn't killed Harvey Parrent.

"How do you know?" Dolf asked.

"I'd as soon not say just yet," Old John hedged.

"That won't do," Dolf told him.

So Hedley related what Baker had told him in his letter.

"I'll be damned," Dolf said. "I came close to shootin' Dwan the first time I ran into him up on the lake. I'm glad I didn't. He's turnin' out to be not half-bad."

Hedley's eyes held Dolf's in a level gaze. "What're you plannin' to do about Twead? I wouldn't blame yuh if yuh went over 'n' gut-shot him."

"I dunno," Dolf said. "I'll sleep on it. He ain't apt to be leavin' before spring."

But he did. He disappeared that night. They didn't miss him until the next day.

"Where the hell could he have gone?" Quillen asked anyone who might offer a guess.

"Might be over at Goldie's," Old John allowed, "but from what I gather, he'd need a bundle to buy his way back inta Goldie's good graces. If he took a bundle over there, we'd probably find him in the Yukon come breakup. I think he's got some injuns to take him up to Ft. Reliance. He can try to get a dog team out over Chilkoot from there. Rough goin', but it's been done."

"I'll check the Skookum Two," Dolf said. "As soon as LaBrae gets over here, I'm takin' a posse over there. No sense in arrestin' Turk, though, and if Blackie was still alive they'd have been over for Doc by now. But I just want to give them the word that Uncle Sam's long arm is up here now."

By the time Dolf's posse got over to Goldley, Turk had had a small taste of miners' law. Some of the boys from the diggins had payed a visit, and a miners' meeting layed on fifty lashes to Turk and ten to Goldie on general principles. When Dolf made known the fact that he was a U.S. deputy marshal, Goldie squawked, "I'm preferrin' charges against those miners."

Dolf only grinned. "Really?" he asked. "Do tell."

Dwan had been in good shape the day after Doc sewed him up, then began to have fevers and was sick to his stomach several times.

"What's the matter with him?" Margaret asked Doc.

"Dunno," Doc said. "The fevers are normal. About the other, it's hard to tell. Maybe the morphine didn't agree with him."

When he was lucid, Dwan was pathetically grateful to Margaret for nursing him. When he was delirious, he thought she was his mother and wanted her to hold his hand. Once he said, "Don't put out the light, Maw. I'm skeered o' the dark." He said that during the brightest part of the short arctic day. For all his background, Margaret pitied him infinitely. And having him to nurse took her mind off of her own appalling unhappiness.

Dolf, of course, couldn't help but notice her pensive moods and withdrawal, and certainly her lack of interest in making love. He knew that women were subject to such strange phases, having been married before. He was the soul of consideration, which caused her to feel guilty, aggravating her turmoil all the more. She learned then that he would never come to her demandingly when she was unresponsive, and loved him all the more for that. But it did not alter her resolve to free him.

Eventually she had to tell him of the new child on the way. The sudden joy in his expression almost convinced her she had wrongly judged his true feeling. But her confidence didn't last, and she was again plunged into black uncertainty and depression. Only her responsibility to Rudy Dwan temporarily allowed her to dwell on something else. Since he naturally sensed her mood, Dolf began to spend more time at Doc's or with his nose in a book. However, he was always tender and considerate toward his Maggie.

Deeply puzzled and hurt by her attitude, he lacked the words to draw out her inner agony. He had learned from a sad life to be patient and hope for the best. Never once did he reprove Margaret, even inwardly.

CHAPTER 17

ON Christmas Day young Henry D. took his first steps by himself. Mama Borealis was prouder than anyone.

"He only nine munt old," she kept marveling.

The event almost restored the old cheerfulness in the cabin. But that night Margaret lost their second child. Dolf roused Doc and brought him over. On the way he asked Doc, "What do you suppose caused it?"

"Something's been eatin' her," Doc guessed. "You got any idea what? Sometimes they just don't want a kid."

Dolf told Doc of her strange moodiness.

"I'll see if she'll talk to me," his friend reassured him. "Sometimes gals unburden on the old Doc here."

At least it raised Dolf's spirits for a while. Later, when Margaret was in bed resting, Doc confided to Dolf, "She didn't say a word."

It was Dolf's worst winter since the prison years. The men put in many evenings playing penny ante poker, cautiously accepting Dwan into the circle. "He's a cheerful scoundrel," Doc admitted one night after Dwan had turned in. Rudy was even living with Doc. "I'm beginning to like the cuss," Doc added.

"The trouble with Rudy," Old John said, "was named Shootin' Shep Thompson. Dolf had the medicine fer that. Rudy has a habit of gettin' in bad company. Best thing that happened to him up here was gettin' shot so he'd get away from Goldie's crowd. I'm thinkin' of givin' him a job in the store till spring. He says he's goin' back to Ft. Belton then. Even plannin' to take Ave along so he can go to school before he's too old. Waddya think of that, Jack?"

"I know. I don't mind. The boy can use it if he can stand it. Rudy sure took a shine to him since Ave saved his neck. I think it might be good fer both of 'em. Do the kid good to see some of the rest of the world. Besides, Ave might be a good example for Rudy." He laughed.

It had been a winter of discontent for Goldie. After his dressing down at the hands of the miners, many of them shunned his place, perhaps for fear of individual retaliation on them. Goldie was sorry he'd ever tried the venture and planned to go back to Juneau in the spring, not realizing that his inability to throttle his blind avarice was all that had prevented his venture from being the bonanza he'd lusted for.

But before I go, he thought, I'm gonna have a crack at the gold goin' outa here. If I can make a big haul, it ain't gonna be Juneau for me. Maybe South America.

Since losing Dwan, Goldie had been grooming Turk as his segundo. Another useful tool fell into his hands in the person of Swede Larson, the *River Queen*'s engineer. Swede liked Goldie's girls. In fact, he spent more time over at the Skookum Two than he did on board the *River Queen*, even though it was a fifty-mile hike over. Goldie carefully sounded him out on joining his scheme. Swede needed more money than he had to keep seeing Goldie's girls. The little conman saw that he got it. When Swede was suitably in debt, Goldie laid his cards on the table.

"Why not?" Swede agreed. "I could use a big score. I don't owe anything to Barlow, and sure not to Brown and Shadley. They're through up here anyhow, whether they know it or not. Word about Twead has got around. One of the boys over at St. John says he knew Twead even before he went to Montana. He cleaned out the outfit he worked for in San Francisco and did time in Folsom for it."

"I ain't surprised," Goldie said.

He laid out his plan for Turk and Larson. "The spring clean-up'll go out on the *Ira Baker* for sure, since nobody trusts Brown and Shadley anymore; in fact, there ain't no Brown and Shadley since Twead pulled out, just Captain Barlow, and you said even Barlow's pullin' his freight as soon as he hits St.

Michael. Morgette'll go along to guard the cleanup, and probably some others. It's a cinch they won't let any of us on board, so we'll take the *River Queen* and jump 'em somewhere, maybe while they're takin' on wood."

"Suppose Barlow don't wanna leave the same time as the *Ira Baker?*" Larson inquired.

Goldie laughed. "Then we'll just hafta borrow his boat. I've got one of the boys that used to pilot on the Mississippi before he figured out gamblers made better dough. You can run the machinery. What the hell do we need Barlow for in that case?"

"There'll be some shootin' fer sure," Larson allowed.

"We'll handle the shootin'. If we pick off Morgette first, we may do the only shootin'. Better yet, I'd like to see him put outa the way before then. I've had some of the boys prowlin' around on the lookout for a chance at him. Too bad he didn't drown when Hoonah Sam cut him loose in that boat."

Margaret had been questioning the soundness of her suspicions about Dolf's feelings for Victoria Wheat. He had never directed a harsh word at her during the whole period of her withdrawal. This, more than anything, made her suspect she'd been woefully wrong, but it also made it hard to admit the root of her conduct, especially to Dolf. She hated to admit it to herself. Dolf had never once hinted he might be thinking of leaving Alaska. In fact, the country seemed to suit him remarkably well. When talk came up of Ave's going outside to school, Dolf mentioned their need to eventually arrange something like that for Henry.

"Are you planning on settling here permanently?" she asked.

"Why not, if it suits you? The states are getting too settled up. Besides, Thunder and Lightning are makin' me and Doc rich. Old Skookum Doc is even thinkin' of staying here permanent."

This didn't sound to her like a man planning to desert her someday. Her spirits rose after this conversation.

I've been a jealous fool, she chided herself. But I'll make it up to him.

Two events livened up the late winter. Mama Borealis found a husband from a village on the other side of the Yukon. He'd been over cutting wood all winter at St. John. As spring approached and the ice breakup would soon cut him off from his people—who would leave for their summer migration—Mama had to choose between him and life with the Morgettes. She tearfully chose to go with her man.

"Mama never forget Maggie 'n' Henry, her two baby," she said, hugging them both. She and Maggie both cried. Henry, recognizing that something was upsetting them, cried too.

The second event was Henry's first birthday. Margaret wanted him to have a party and went to great pains to arrange a proper one. She invited their inner circle of friends. She made a cake. Ice cream was no problem since it was still cold enough that canned milk mixed with vanilla and placed outdoors in a pan made it in no time at all. She had cookies, coffee, and a potent punch that proved popular with the men. Even Dolf exceeded his usual "one" by several.

That night Margaret came to Dolf warm, yielding, and hungry for his old familiar warmth.

"I'm home again," she whispered afterward.

"Where have you been?" he asked, hoping to learn what had been troubling her.

"I don't know," she said. "But I'm glad to be home."

Then, realizing how unfair she was being, she confessed her whole problem to him. He was quiet for sometime, cursing himself for not having recognized what was wrong.

"I love you, Maggie," he told her. "I'll never love anyone else—I know that. I hope you can believe me."

"I believe you," she whispered.

The old cheerfulness again pervaded the cabin. As the days grew longer, the eaves began to drip, and it was good to crack the windows a little to listen to it—a sure sign of spring. The men formed a betting pool on when the ice would go out, wagering a dollar a chance. It had been a cold winter, and the ice was unusually thick, going out later than usual. When it did go, it went swiftly. Long leads had appeared for several days with water on top of the ice. Ominous booming could be heard from time to time as the spring melt from the hills was raising the water beneath, pushing the ice upward.

One day, unsuspecting, Dolf was out with his shotgun on the hill above St. John, hunting grouse. He started down and stopped to watch the spectacle. Huge blocks of ice suddenly upended, climbing onto others, accompanied by thunderous snapping and stupendous grinding noises. Suddenly the whole Sky Pilot River was in motion, water flooding high above the ice. From his position, Dolf could see the danger approaching before anyone below would realize it. He thought of yelling, but the distance was too great. Instead he began to run.

A monstrous ice jam had formed in the bend of the river below the village. Water was backing up at an alarming rate, boiling from beneath the surface. A huge black flood of it was sweeping down from above on top of the ice, forced up by the jam downstream. Dolf reached the village in time to see his cabin awash up to the eaves in this backwater. It broke loose and swirled lazily out into the cold whirling mass. To his horror, he recognized Margaret with Henry in her arms precariously riding on the roof. How they'd got there he couldn't imagine. He frantically looked around for the nearest boat, realizing that no one could swim in water that cold. It paralyzed the diaphragm, preventing breathing.

Someone else had spotted the predicament of the two on the roof and was frantically shoving a boat into the flood further down. Dolf raced to join whoever it was, but he was too late. He saw Rudy Dwan laying to the oars, stroking like a madman. Dolf was too alarmed to be surprised at Rudy's reaction. He watched the race as Rudy closed on the floating cabin, finally ramming the bow against it. Margaret leaped into the boat clutching Henry. Dolf heaved a sigh of relief—too soon. Something below had given way, and the water suddenly accelerated, sweeping the small boat away like a wood chip. Dolf felt like closing his eyes. He could see what was going to happen. The river was sweeping against the jam and disappearing down the funnel that had opened beneath the ice pile, sucking everything downward like a gigantic drainpipe. Rudy was laying to the oars like a maniac as they were drawn inexorably nearer to this deadly trap; then, in an instant, they and the boat disappeared somewhere in the icy depths.

Others had watched this horrid sight as well. The Morgette cabin had been closest to the stream, though in an ordinary year it would certainly have been well above flood level. Doc watched helplessly, stranded on his own cabin roof. His cabin, however, remained precariously in place as the flood started to ebb. Dolf and others ran futilely downstream along the hillside, hoping to see the boat come up through an air hole, or perhaps to see some of the occupants somehow struggle out onto the ice, but their hopes were doomed to disappointment. Dolf, followed by Jim Too, worked his way clear down to the Yukon, but saw nothing of the lost party or the boat. He was still too numbed by the horrifying sight to feel the full sense of his loss.

CHAPTER 18

DOLF was stricken for days, without appetite or enthusiasm. If he hadn't been inured to numbing losses in the past, he might have ended it all. The thought crossed his mind more than once. But he always remembered his responsibility to his family back in Idaho and to the people here who still looked to him for law and order. Jim Too searched for days for his missing people, sometimes coming to Dolf whining dolefully, as though to ask him where they were.

Dolf helped Doc clean up his place, then moved in with him. Doc realized that it was useless to try to comfort his friend with words. Soon the need for action would be the best medicine for him. All the ice was gone and spring cleanup progressing rapidly up at the diggings. The earliest to finish up were already beginning to filter in, depositing their new wealth with Hedley for transport outside. Many were planning to pull out with him for home. Most returned to their rich claims, looking forward to even greater wealth.

Goldie had a constant watch on the preparations of the *Ira Baker*. When it pulled out, he put his plan into action, commandeering the *River Queen* with the full battalion of his thugs. He had deserted his girls, not telling them that he wouldn't be back.

"They'll make out," he chortled to Turk. "Probably be the richest prospectors up here after another winter. They can keep the damn place."

The *Ira Baker* was in the Yukon well downstream when Hedley spied the *River Queen* following.

"Now what the hell is Barlow up to?" he muttered to Dolf who was in the pilot house with him. "He wasn't aimin' ta pull out for a week."

He laid his telescope on the other boat and scanned it

closely. The sight of Goldie and some of his crew of cutthroats answered his question.

"Take a look," he invited Dolf.

"I can imagine what they're after," Dolf said. "Can we stay ahead of them?"

"Only till we have to put in for wood."

"Looks like we're in for a fight."

"I wouldn't bet on it," Old John cackled. "I think they're in for a little surprise."

They got it just as he mentioned it. The sound of a muffled explosion reached them across the water. A churning cloud of oily black smoke shot from the *River Queen*'s stacks. The steamer began to list sharply, drifting dead in the water. Dolf laid the glass on it again.

"They're gettin' into the lifeboats."

Hedley took the glass. "There ain't nobody back there I'd help even if they didn't have boats. I don't see Barlow. They musta stole his boat."

"You goin' back?" Dolf asked.

"Hell no. Let LaBrae handle 'em. Maybe them miners'll get guts enough to hang 'em this time."

"What do you suppose happened?" Dolf inquired.

"Well," Old John said, "I figured I owed Brown and Shadley one. So I loaned 'em some cord wood. Only I forgot to mention that I had some of it drilled out and filled with blasting powder, then plugged it back up. Ain't that a shame?"

He threw back his head and cackled wickedly. Dolf recalled the Indians Old John had hanged without compunction, so he forbore asking how he'd been sure no one innocent would be hurt. By now he knew Old John's philosophy, the hard unyielding side of him. He knew Hedley hadn't cared who got hurt as long as he got even.

They found the *Idaho* in port when they reached St. Michael and transferred their treasure on board. They also learned something that surprised them both. Twead had somehow made his way down the river that winter and had left on the first ship out a week before.

"For where?" Hedley asked.

"I dunno," the clerk at the B & S store told him. "The ship was bound for Frisco."

That changed Dolf's plan to return upriver. There was really nothing left for him there. He wrote Doc a note and sent it back with the new captain of the *Ira Baker*. Then he boarded the *Idaho*, headed south with Hedley.

"I still owe Harvey Parrent's family Twead's hide," Dolf told Old John. "I'll catch him sooner or later."

Dolf carried a weight heavier than the gold with him. Poor lost Maggie and Henry were on his mind constantly. He'd searched the riverbanks, islands, and sandbars for days before he'd left, but if there was a trace of them, he'd always been in the wrong place. He'd inquired of every Indian or white he'd met on the river.

At night a vision of her came to him in his sleep, holding Henry out to him. He'd sit up, reaching out, but the shards of the bright dream would shatter about him, leaving him alone in the darkness. He thought, It's better than *never* seeing them again.

The *Idaho* put into Dyea, dropped off Old John, and picked up Dolf's horse Wowakan. Old John solemnly shook hands with him at the gangplank. "We'll miss you, Dolf. Come back someday. Alaska needs you."

Dolf looked back painfully as Dyea gradually dissolved in the distance; only the timeless glaciers towering brightly above it in the cloudless blue were still in sight.

The remembrance of those happy times at Dyea, the best days of his life—and realization that they could never return —overwhelmed him.

EPILOGUE

Margaret's first sensation was of being terribly cold, colder than she'd ever been in her life. She moved slowly, gradually able to rise. She'd held Henry beside her in a death hug. She looked around, dazed. They were on an ice floe in the midst of a vast sea of them. The shoreline, marked by its tree fringe, was at least a half mile away on either side.

I'll never make it, she thought. What will happen to Henry?

The next thing she remembered was being in a hut bundled in blankets with a warm fire burning. She saw Mama Borealis's face swim into focus above her.

"Where am I?" she asked, thinking perhaps she was really dead and in another world. "Where's Henry?"

"Henry okay," Mama assured her. "You be okay. Inchen fish my beeby outa river. Wat happen?"

But Margaret couldn't tell her. She lapsed into delirium, hovering at the edge of death with pneumonia for a week. Another month passed before she was able to get up. By then the Indians had carried Margaret and Henry with them at least one hundred miles to their favorite salmon-fishing grounds.

Margaret knew that Dolf had planned to leave temporarily, guarding the spring cleanup at least as far as St. Michael. She did not know that he thought she and Henry were dead, or that he had spent frantic distraught weeks searching for them before he'd admitted that to himself and finally left.

"Why didn't you send Dolf word right away?" Margaret asked Mama Borealis.

"Ice goin' out. No good boat." Mama shrugged. "Not know if Maggie live yet." They were all practical reasons to her mind. Mama's tribe was too poor to have very good boats. Even if they had, putting any small boat in the heavily running ice would have been extremely dangerous. They had rescued Margaret in a precarious footrace across the floating ice.

Margaret appreciated the native woman's rare sensitivity in wanting to spare Dolf the anguish of possibly having his hopes raised, only to come and find Maggie dead after all. She wondered if Mama would have returned Henry to Dolf if she'd died. She tried to put herself in Mama's place and wasn't at all sure what she'd have done. Well, she wasn't going to die. And the frustration of being unable to get word to Dolf was eating at her.

She was still too weak to take care of herself and Henry, so it was a case of getting someone else to carry a letter to Dolf. They were finally able to flag down a boat full of prospectors headed down to the Sky Pilot diggins. Several other boats had passed quickly, their occupants fearful of Indian treachery. She borrowed some writing materials from the people who stopped, and addressed a message to either Dolf or Doc.

Weeks passed with no reply, though at first her hopes were high. She envisioned even the *Ira Baker* being sent up to get her. Finally an Indian brought word back to her. He carried her original message, the envelope now crumpled and grimy but still sealed. Her original message was scribbled over in pencil: "Both these gents went back to the states."

Margaret's spirits sunk. Why hadn't Dolf returned? A terrible suspicion entered her mind. If he thought I was dead, he could go back to her. Suppose I follow him and find out they're married?

She was now in a panic to reach St. John herself. She knew that Old John had been planning to bring Elsie up and that they would probably be back by now. She wanted to talk to Elsie particularly, since they shared a problem in common. They were Indians married to successful white men. Beyond that, she had no doubt but what she could get money from either Old John or Elsie for passage outside.

As she thought this over, her sense of urgency abated. Maybe, she reasoned, I should take Henry and go back to my own people *where we belong*. That would be fairer to Dolf. In time he'd forget.

But, if she did that, she'd have to depend on Elsie and Old John to keep the secret that she was alive. Surely Hedley, being a man, would send Dolf a letter and spill the beans to him. Because that was true, she resolved to somehow go down to St. John and secretly see Elsie alone first. She didn't know what her plans would be after that. She was a woman with a terrible dilemma; her heart and mind were in two worlds totally alien to each other, and she lacked the sophistication to even analyze the problem, much less resolve it.

Broken Ranks

Hiram King

The Civil War just ended. For one group of black men, hope for a new life comes in the form of a piece of paper, a government handbill urging volunteers to join the new Negro Cavalry, which will soon become the famous Tenth Cavalry Regiment. But trouble begins for the recruits long before they can even reach their training camp. First they have to get from St. Louis to Fort Leavenworth, Kansas, a hard journey through hostile, ex-Confederate territory, surrounded by vengeful white men who don't like the idea of these recruits having guns. The army hires Ples Butler, a grim, black gunfighter, to get the recruits to Fort Leavenworth safely, and he will do his job . . . even if it means riding through Hell.

___4872-8 $5.99 US/$6.99 CAN

BENEATH A
WHISKEY SKY
TRACY KNIGHT

Escaping the past is no easy feat. Just ask Sim McCracken. Sim is a jaded, weary gunslinger with a whole packsaddle worth of secrets and shame, who wants nothing more than to forge a new life. That's why he spared the life of the young pastor he was hired to kill. But that hasn't made the land baron who hired him for the job too happy. Before Sim has a chance to make a clean escape, another secret from his past catches up with him—a retarded brother named Charles, whom Sim hasn't seen since they were children. Sim has to travel across Missouri to escort Charles to a hospital, with his past breathing down his neck the whole way—and with murderous pursuers just one step behind him.

___4883-3 $4.50 US/$5.50 CAN

Man From Wolf River

John D. Nesbitt

Owen Felver is just passing through. He is on his way from the Wolf River down to the Laramie Mountains for some summer wages. He makes his camp outside of Cameron, Wyoming, and rides in for a quick beer. But it isn't quick enough. While he is there he sees pretty, young Jenny—and the puffed-up gent trying to get rude with her. What else can he do but step in and defend her? Right after that some pretty tough thugs start to make it clear Felver isn't all too welcome around town. Trouble is, the more they tell him to move on—and the more he sees of Jenny—the more he wants to stay. He knows they have something to hide, but he has no idea just how awful it is—or how far they will go to keep it hidden.

___4871-X $4.50 US/$5.50 CAN

Dorchester Publishing Co., Inc.
P.O. Box 6640
Wayne, PA 19087-8640

WILD BILL: GUN LAW

JUDD COLE

Leland Langford, owner of the Overland Stage and Freighting Company, has a dangerous job and he knows there is only one man for it, the legendary Wild Bill Hickok. Leland knows that only Wild Bill can ensure that a gold shipment travels safely from the Black Hills to Denver. But there is an even more important part of Bill's mission. Bill has to break up one of the cleverest and most vicious rings of thieves ever to terrorize the West, and send one message loud and clear: Steal gold from the U.S. Treasury and you'll face the harshest law in the West . . . gun law.

___4874-4 $3.99 US/$4.99 CAN

MEN BEYOND THE LAW

These three short novels showcase Max Brand doing what he does best: exploring the wild, often dangerous life beyond the constraints of cities, beyond the reach of civilization . . . beyond the law. Whether he's a desperate man fleeing the tragic results of a gunfight, an innocent young man who stumbles onto the loot from a bank robbery, or the gentle giant named Bull Hunter—one of Brand's most famous characters—each protagonist is out on his own, facing two unknown frontiers: the Wild West . . . and his own future.

___4873-6 $4.50 US/$5.50 CAN

Dorchester Publishing Co., Inc.
P.O. Box 6640
Wayne, PA 19087-8640

Please add $2.50 for shipping and handling for the first book and $.75 for each book thereafter. NY, NYC, and PA residents, please add appropriate sales tax. No cash, stamps, or C.O.D.s. All orders shipped within 6 weeks via postal service book rate. Canadian orders require $2.50 extra postage and must be paid in U.S. dollars through a U.S. banking facility.

Name_____
Address_____
City_____State_____Zip_____
I have enclosed $ _____ in payment for the checked book(s).
Payment <u>must</u> accompany all orders. ☐ Please send a free catalog.
CHECK OUT OUR WEBSITE! www.dorchesterpub.com

LAURAN PAINE

THE KILLER GUN

It is no ordinary gun. It is specially designed to help its owner kill a man. George Mars has customized a Colt revolver so it will fire when it is on half cock, saving the time it takes to pull back the hammer before firing. But then the gun is stolen from Mars's shop. Mars has engraved his name on it but, as the weapon passes from hand to hand, owner to owner, killer to killer, his identity becomes as much of a mystery as why possession of the gun skews the odds in any duel. And the legend of the killer gun grows with each newly slain man.

___4875-2 $4.50 US/$5.50 CAN

WILDERNESS

Fang & Claw
David Thompson

To survive in the untamed wilderness a man needs all the friends he can get. No one can battle the continual dangers on his own. Even a fearless frontiersman like Nate King needs help now and then and he's always ready to give it when it's needed. So when an elderly Shoshone warrior comes to Nate asking for help, Nate agrees to lend a hand. The old warrior knows he doesn't have long to live and he wants to die in the remote canyon where his true love was killed many years before, slain by a giant bear straight out of Shoshone myth. No Shoshone will dare accompany the old warrior, so he and Nate will brave the dreaded canyon alone. And as Nate soon learns the hard way, some legends are far better left undisturbed.

___4862-0 $3.99 US/$4.99 CAN

THE BLOODY QUARTER

LES SAVAGE, JR.

Paul Hagar has always had hard luck. He's drifted through the Southwest, trying his hand at a few different things, but always with no success. Then it looks like his luck has changed. He has a chance to file for land in the most important quarter section in all of Converse County, Wyoming. Known as the Bloody Quarter, the strip serves as a gateway for the surrounding ranchers to summer graze their herds in the high country. But it is called the Bloody Quarter for a reason—some pretty ruthless ranchers are willing to do just about anything to control it. Even commit murder. Paul Hagar's luck might have changed, all right . . . but for the worse.

___4863-9 $4.50 US/$5.50 CAN

Gary McCarthy
THE BUFFALO HUNTERS

Thomas Atherton is a young stable master from Massachusetts who has always dreamed of leaving Boston behind and heading west across the great frontier. When he meets the legendary Buffalo Bill Cody at his famous Wild West Show, Thomas decides the time has finally come to make his dream a reality. He sees his chance when he hears about a $5,000 reward offered to the first man to find a surviving herd of the nearly extinct buffalo. And so he sets out to test his mettle on a buffalo hunt. But he will soon find that taming horses is nothing compared with taming the prairie and the rugged mountains beyond—or surviving run-ins with vicious outlaws and rustlers.

___4884-1 $3.99 US/$4.99 CAN